PENGUIN BOOKS
A FLIGHT OF PIGEONS

Ruskin Bond was born in Kasauli in 1934, and grew up in Jamnagar, Dehradun, New Delhi and Simla. As a young man, he spent four years in the Channel Islands and London. He returned to India in 1955, and has never left the country since. His first novel, *The Room on the Roof*, received the John Llewellyn Rhys Prize, awarded to a Commonwealth writer under thirty for 'a work of outstanding literary merit'. He has, since, published over thirty-five books, including the novellas *A Flight of Pigeons* and *Delhi Is Not Far*, and several collections of short stories. He received a Sahitya Akademi Award in 1993, and the Padma Shri in 1999.

He lives in Landour, Mussoorie, with his extended family.

ALSO BY RUSKIN BOND

Fiction

The Night Train at Deoli and Other Stories
Time Stops at Shamli and Other Stories
The Room on the Roof & Vagrants in the Valley
Our Trees Still Grow in Dehra
Delhi Is Not Far: The Best of Bond
Collected Fiction (1995–1996)
Strangers in the Night: Two Novellas
Season of Ghosts
Friends in Small Places
When Darkness Falls and Other Stories

Non-Fiction

Rain in the Mountains
Scenes from a Writer's Life
The Lamp Is Lit
The Little Book of Comfort

Anthologies (edited)

Indian Ghost Stories
Indian Railway Stories
Indian Classical Love Stories

Puffin

Ruskin Bond's Treasury of Stories for Children
Panther's Moon and Other Stories
The Room on the Roof

Ruskin Bond

A Flight of Pigeons

PENGUIN BOOKS

PENGUIN ENTERPRISE
Published by the Penguin Group
Penguin Books India Pvt. Ltd, 11 Community Centre, Panchsheel Park, New Delhi 110 017, India
Penguin Group (USA) Inc., 375 Hudson Street, New York, New York 10014, USA
Penguin Group (Canada), 90 Eglinton Avenue East, Suite 700, Toronto, Ontario, M4P 2Y3, Canada (a division of Pearson Penguin Canada Inc.)
Penguin Books Ltd, 80 Strand, London WC2R 0RL, England
Penguin Ireland, 25 St Stephen's Green, Dublin 2, Ireland (a division of Penguin Books Ltd)
Penguin Group (Australia), 707 Collins Street, Melbourne, Victoria 3008, Australia (a division of Pearson Australia Group Pty Ltd)
Penguin Group (NZ), 67 Apollo Drive, Rosedale, Auckland 0632, New Zealand (a division of Pearson New Zealand Ltd)
Penguin Group (South Africa) (Pty) Ltd, 24 Sturdee Avenue, Rosebank, Johannesburg 2196, South Africa

Penguin Books Ltd, Registered Offices: 80 Strand, London WC2R 0RL, England

First published in Viking by Penguin Books India 2002
Penguin Books India 2007

14 13 12 11 10 9 8

ISBN 9780143063223

Typeset in New Baskerville by S.R. Enterprises, New Delhi
Printed at Rashtriya Printers, New Delhi

Contents

Introduction .... *vii*
Prologue 1
At the Church 6
Lala Ramjimal 12
In Lala's House 17
A Change of Name 26
Another Nawab 34
Caught! 39
Javed Khan 43
Guests of the Pathan 49
Pilloo's Fate 55
Further Alarms 58
Another Proposal 66
On Show 72

The Rains 81
White Pigeons 87
The Impatience of Javed Khan 92
A Visit from Kothiwali 97
The Fall of Delhi 106
Behind the Curtain 110
The Battle of Bichpuri 114
In Flight Again 120
The Final Journey 125
Notes 134

Introduction

I remember my father telling me the story of a girl who had a recurring dream in which she witnessed the massacre of the congregation in a small church in northern India. A couple of years later she found herself in an identical church in Shahjahanpur, where she was witness to the same horrifying scenes which had now become a reality.

My father was born in Shahjahanpur and had probably heard the tale from his soldier father who had been stationed there afterwards. Whether the girl in question was Ruth Labadoor (or possibly Lemaistre) or someone else, one cannot say at this point in time. But Ruth's story is true. She survived the killings and her subsequent ordeal, and lived to tell her story to more than one person; mention of it crops up time and again in old records and accounts of the 'Mutiny' of 1857.

In retelling the tale for today's reader I attempted to bring out the common humanity of most of the people involved—for in times of conflict and inter-religious or racial hatred, there are always a few (just a few) who are prepared to come to the aid of those unable to defend themselves.

I published this account as a novella about thirty years ago. I feel it still has some relevance today, when communal strife and religious intolerance threaten the lives and livelihood of innocent, law-abiding people. It was Pascal who wrote: 'Men never do evil so completely and cheerfully as when they do it from religious conviction.' Fortunately for civilization, there are exceptions.

Ruskin Bond
March 2002

Prologue

The revolt broke out at Meerut on the 10th of May, at the beginning of a very hot and oppressive summer. The sepoys shot down their English officers; there was rioting and looting in the city; the jail was broken open, and armed convicts descended on English families living in the city and cantonment, setting fire to houses and killing the inmates. Several mutinous regiments marched to Delhi, their principal rallying-point, where the peaceable, poetry-loving Emperor Bahadur Shah suddenly found himself the figurehead of the revolt.

The British Army, which had been cooling off in Shimla, began its long march to Delhi. But meanwhile, the conflict had spread to other cities. And on the 30th of May there was much excitement in the magistrate's office at Shahjahanpur, some 250 miles east of Delhi.

A bungalow in the cantonment, owned by the Redmans, an Anglo-Indian family, had been set on fire during the night. The Redmans had been able to escape, but most of their property was looted or destroyed. A familiar figure had been seen flitting around the grounds that night; and Javed Khan, a Rohilla Pathan, well-known to everyone in the city, was arrested on suspicion of arson and brought before the magistrate.

Javed Khan was a person of some importance in the bazaars of Shahjahanpur. He had a reputation for agreeing to undertake any exploit of a dangerous nature, provided the rewards were high. He had been brought in by the authorities for a number of offences. But Javed knew the English law, and challenged the court to produce witnesses. None came forward to identify him as the man who had been seen running from the blazing bungalow. The case was adjourned until further evidence could be collected. When Javed left the courtroom, it was difficult to tell whether he was being escorted by the police or whether he was escorting them. Before leaving the room, he bowed contemptuously to Mr Ricketts, the magistrate, and said: '*My* witnesses will be produced tomorrow, whether you will have them or not.'

* * * * * *

The burning of the Redmans' bungalow failed to alert the small English community in Shahjahanpur to a sense of danger. Meerut was far away, and the *Moffusilite*, the local news sheet, carried very little news of the disturbances. The army officers made their rounds without noticing anything unusual, and the civilians went to their offices. In the evening they met in the usual fashion, to eat and drink and dance.

On the 30th of May it was Dr Bowling's turn as host. In his drawing-room, young Lieutenant Scott strummed a guitar, while Mrs Bowling sang a romantic ballad. Four army officers sat down to a game of whist, while Mrs Ricketts, Mr Jenkins, the Collector, and Captain James, discussed the weather over a bottle of Exshaw's whisky.

Only the Labadoors had any foreboding of trouble. They were not at the party.

Mr Labadoor was forty-two, his wife thirty-eight. Their daughter, Ruth, was a pretty girl, with raven black hair and dark, lustrous eyes. She had left Mrs Shield's school at Fatehgarh only a fortnight before, because her mother felt she would be safer at home.

Mrs Labadoor's father had been a French adventurer who had served in the Maratha army; her mother came from a well-known Muslim family of Rampur. Her name was Mariam. She and her brothers had been brought up as Christians. At eighteen, she married Labadoor, a quiet, unassuming man, who was a clerk in the magistrate's office. He was the grandson of a merchant from Jersey (in the

Channel Islands), and his original Jersey name was Labadu.

While most of the British wives in the cantonment thought it beneath their dignity to gossip with servants, Mariam Labadoor, who made few social calls, enjoyed these conversations of hers. Often they enlivened her day by reporting the juiciest scandals, on which they were always well-informed. But from what Mariam had heard recently, she was convinced that it was only a matter of hours before rioting broke out in the city. News of the events at Meerut had reached the bazaars and sepoy lines, and a fakir, who lived near the River Khannaut, was said to have predicted the end of the English East India Company's rule in the coming months. Mariam made her husband and daughter stay at home the evening of the Bowling's party, and had even suggested that they avoid going to church the next day, Sunday: a surprising request from Mariam, a regular church-goer.

Ruth liked having her way, and insisted on going to church the next day; and her father promised to accompany her.

* * * * * *

The sun rose in a cloudless, shimmering sky, and only those who had risen at dawn had been lucky enough to enjoy the cool breeze that had blown across the river for a brief spell. At seven o'clock the church bell began to toll, and people could be seen making their way towards the small, sturdily built cantonment church. Some, like Mr Labadoor, and his daughter, were on foot, wearing their Sunday clothes. Others came in carriages, or were borne aloft in *dolies* manned by sweating *dolie*-bearers.

St Mary's, the little church in Shahjahanpur, was situated on the southern boundary of the cantonment, near an ancient mango-grove. There were three entrances: one to the south, facing a large compound known as Buller's; another to the west, below the steeple; and the vestry door opening to the north. A narrow staircase led up to the steeple. To the east there were open fields sloping down to the river, cultivated with melon; to the west, lay an open plain bounded by the city; while the parade ground stretched away to the north until it reached the barracks of the sepoys. The bungalows scattered about the side of the parade ground belonged to the regimental officers, Englishmen who had slept soundly, quite unaware of an atmosphere charged with violence.

I will let Ruth take up the story . . .

At the Church

FATHER AND I had just left the house when we saw several sepoys crossing the road, on their way to the river for their morning bath. They stared so fiercely at us that I pressed close to my father and whispered, 'Papa, how strange they look!' But their appearance did not strike him as unusual: the sepoys usually passed that way when going to the River Khannaut, and I suppose Father was used to meeting them on his way to office.

We entered the church from the south porch, and took our seats in the last pew to the right. A number of people had already arrived, but I did not particularly notice who they were. We had knelt down, and were in the middle of the Confession, when we heard a tumult outside and a lot of shouting, that seemed nearer every moment. Everyone in the church got up, and Father left our pew and went and stood at the door, where I joined him.

There were six or seven men on the porch. Their faces were covered up to their noses, and they wore tight loincloths as though they had prepared for a wrestling bout; but they held naked swords in their hands. As soon as they saw us, they sprang forward, and one of them made a cut at us. The sword missed us both and caught the side of the door where it buried itself in the wood. My father had his left hand against the door, and I rushed out from under it, and escaped into the church compound.

A second and third cut were made at my father by the others, both of which caught him on his right cheek. Father tried to seize the sword of one of his assailants, but he caught it high up on the blade, and so firmly, that he lost two fingers from his right hand. These were the only cuts he received; but though he did not fall, he was bleeding profusely. All this time I had stood looking on from the porch, completely bewildered and dazed by what had happened. I remember asking my father what had happened to make him bleed so much.

'Take the handkerchief from my pocket and bandage my face,' he said.

When I had made a bandage from both our handkerchiefs and tied it about his head, he said he wished to go home. I took him by the hand and tried to lead him out of the porch; but we had gone only a few steps when he began to feel faint, and said, 'I can't walk, Ruth. Let us go back to the church.'

* * * * * *

The armed men had made only one rush through the church, and had then gone off through the vestry door. After wounding my father, they had run up the centre of the aisle, slashing right and left. They had taken a cut at Lieutenant Scott, but his mother threw herself over him and received the blow on her ribs; her tight clothes saved her from a serious injury. Mr Ricketts, Mr Jenkins, the Collector, and Mr MacCullam, the Minister, ran out through the vestry.

The rest of the congregation had climbed up to the belfry, and on my father's urging me to do so, I joined them there. We saw Captain James riding up to the church, quite unaware of what was happening. We shouted him a warning, but as he looked up at us, one of the sepoys, who were scattered about on the parade ground, fired at him, and he fell from his horse. Now two other officers came running from the Mess, calling out to the sepoys: 'Oh! children, what are you doing?' They tried to pacify their men, but no one listened to them. They had, however, been popular officers with the sepoys, who did not prevent them from joining us in the turret with their pistols in their hands.

Just then we saw a carriage coming at full speed towards the church. It was Dr Bowling's, and it carried him, his wife and child, and the nanny. The carriage had to cross the parade ground, and they were halfway across when a bullet hit the doctor who was sitting on the coach box. He doubled up in his seat, but did not let go of the reins, and the carriage had almost reached the church, when a sepoy ran up and made a slash at Mrs Bowling, missing her by inches. When the carriage reached the church, some of the officers ran down to help Dr Bowling off the coach box. He struggled in their arms for a while, and was dead when they got him to the ground.

I had come down from the turret with the officers, and now ran to where my father lay. He was sitting against the wall, in a large pool of blood. He did not complain of any pain, but his lips were parched, and he kept his eyes open with an effort. He told me to go home, and to ask Mother to send someone with a cot, or a *dolie*, to carry him back. So much had happened so quickly that I was completely dazed, and though Mrs Bowling and the other women were weeping, there wasn't a tear in my eye. There were two great wounds on my father's face, and I was reluctant to leave him, but to run home and fetch a *dolie* seemed to be the only way in which I could help him.

Leaving him against the stone wall of the church, I ran round to the vestry side and almost fell over Mr Ricketts, who was lying about twelve feet from the vestry door. He had been attacked by an expert and powerful swordsman, whose blow had cut through the trunk from the left shoulder separating the head and right hand from the rest of the body. Sick with horror, I turned from the spot and began running home through Buller's compound.

Nobody met me on the way. No one challenged me, or tried to intercept or molest me. The cantonment seemed empty and deserted; but just as I reached the end of Buller's compound, I saw our house in flames. I stopped at the gate, looking about for my mother, but could not see her anywhere. Granny, too, was missing, and the servants. Then I saw Lala Ramjimal walking down the road towards me.

'Don't worry, my child,' he said. 'Mother, Granny and the others are all safe. Come, I will take you to them.'

There was no question of doubting Lala Ramjimal's intentions. He had held me on his knee when I was a baby, and I had grown up under his eyes. He led me to a hut some thirty yards from our old home. It was a mud house, facing the road, and its door was closed. Lala knocked on the door, but received no answer; then he put his mouth to a chink and whispered, '*Missy-baba* is with me, open the door.'

The door opened, and I rushed into my mother's arms.

'Thank God!' she cried. 'At least one is spared to me.'

'Papa is wounded at the church,' I said. 'Send someone to fetch him.'

Mother looked up at Lala and he could not resist the appeal in her eyes.

'I will go,' he said. 'Do not move from here until I return.'

'You don't know where he is,' I said. 'Let me come with you and help you.'

'No, you must not leave your mother now,' said Lala. 'If you are seen with me, we shall both be killed.'

He returned in the afternoon, after several hours. 'Sahib is dead,' he said, very simply. 'I arrived in time to see him die. He had lost so much blood that it was impossible for him to live. He could not speak and his eyes were becoming glazed, but he looked at me in such a way that I am sure he recognized me . . .'

Lala Ramjimal

Lala left us in the afternoon, promising to return when it grew dark, then he would take us to his own house. He ran a grave risk in doing so, but he had promised us his protection, and he was a man who, once he had decided on taking a certain course of action, could not be shaken from his purpose. He was not a Government servant and owed no loyalties to the British; nor had he conspired with the rebels, for his path never crossed theirs. He had been content always to go about his business (he owned several *dolies* and carriages, which he hired out to Europeans who could not buy their own) in a quiet and efficient manner, and was held in some respect by those he came into contact with; his motives were always personal and if he helped us, it was not because we belonged to the ruling class—my father was probably the most junior officer in Shahjahanpur—but because he had known us for many years, and had grown fond of my mother, who had always treated him as a friend and equal.

I realized that I was now fatherless, and my mother, a widow; but we had no time to indulge in our private sorrow. Our own lives were in constant danger. From our hiding place we could hear the crackling of timber coming from our burning house. The road from the city to the cantonment was in an uproar, with people shouting on all sides. We heard the tramp of men passing up and down the road, just in front of our door; a moan or a sneeze would have betrayed us, and then we would have been at the mercy of the most ruffianly elements from the bazaar, whose swords flashed in the dazzling sunlight.

There were eight of us in the little room: Mother, Granny, myself; my cousin, Anet; my mother's half-brother, Pilloo, who was about my age, and his mother; our servants, Champa and Lado; as well as two of our black and white spaniels, who had followed close on Mother's heels when she fled from the house.

The mud hut in which we were sheltering was owned by Tirloki, a mason who had helped build our own house. He was well-known to us. Weeks before the outbreak, when Mother used to gossip with her servants and others about the possibility of trouble in Shahjahanpur, Tirloki had been one of those who had offered his house for shelter should she ever be in need of it. And Mother, as a precaution, had accepted his offer, and taken the key from him.

Mother afterwards told me that as she sat on the veranda that morning one of the gardener's sons had come running to her in great haste and had cried out: 'Mutiny broken out, sahib and *missy-baba* killed!' Hearing that we had both been killed, Mother's first impulse was to throw herself into the nearest well; but Granny caught hold of her, and begged her not to be rash, saying, 'And what will become of the rest of us if you do such a thing?' And so she had gone across the road, followed by the others, and had entered Tirloki's house and chained the door from within.

* * * * * *

We were shut up in the hut all day, expecting, at any moment, to be discovered and killed. We had no food at all, but we could not have eaten any had it been there. My father gone, our future appeared a perfect void, and we found it difficult to talk. A hot wind blew through the cracks in the door, and our throats were parched. Late in the afternoon, a *chatty* of cold water was let down to us from a tree outside a window at the rear of the hut. This was an act of compassion on the part of a man called Chinta, who had worked for us as a labourer when our bungalow was being built.

At about ten o'clock, Lala returned, accompanied by Dhani, our old bearer. He proposed to take us to his own house. Mother hesitated to come out into the open, but Lala assured her that the roads were quite clear now, and there was little fear of our being molested. At last, she agreed to go.

We formed two batches. Lala led the way with a drawn sword in one hand, his umbrella in the other. Mother and Anet and I followed, holding each other's hands. Mother had thrown over us a counterpane which she had been carrying with her when she left the house. We avoided the main road, making our way round the sweeper settlement, and reached Lala's house after a fifteen-minute walk. On our arrival there, Lala offered us a bed to sit upon, while he squatted down on the ground with his legs crossed.

Mother had thrown away her big bunch of keys as we left Tirloki's house. When I asked her why she had done so, she pointed to the smouldering ruins of our bungalow and said: 'Of what possible use could they be to us now?'

The bearer, Dhani, arrived with the second batch, consisting of dear Granny, Pilloo and his mother, and Champa and Lado, and the dogs. There were eight of us in Lala's small house; and, as far as I could tell, his own family was as large as ours.

We were offered food, but we could not eat. We lay down for the night—Mother, Granny and I on the bed, the rest on the ground. And in the darkness, with my face against my mother's bosom, I gave vent to my grief and wept bitterly. My mother wept, too, but silently, and I think she was still weeping when at last I fell asleep.

In Lala's House

Lala Ramjimal's family consisted of himself, his wife, mother, aunt and sister. It was a house of women, and our unexpected arrival hadn't changed that. It must indeed have been a test of the Lala's strength and patience, with twelve near-hysterical females on his hands!

His family, of course, knew who we were, because Lala's mother and aunt used to come and draw water from our well, and offer bel leaves at the little shrine near our house. They were at first shy of us; and we, so immersed in our own predicament, herded together in a corner of the house, looked at each other's faces and wept. Lala's wife would come and serve us food in platters made of stitched leaves. We ate once in twenty-four hours, a little after noon, but we were satisfied with this one big meal.

The house was an ordinary mud building, consisting of four flat-roofed rooms, with a low veranda in the front, and a courtyard at the back. It was small and unpretentious, occupied by a family of small means.

Lala's wife was a young woman, short in stature, with a fair complexion. We didn't know her name, because it is not customary for a husband or wife to call the other by name; but her mother-in-law would address her as *dulhan*, or bride.

Ramjimal himself was a tall, lean man, with a long moustache. His speech was always very polite, like that of most Kayasthas but he had an air of determination about him that was rare in others.

On the second day of our arrival, I overheard his mother speaking to him: 'Lalaji, you have made a great mistake in bringing these *Angrezans* into our house. What will people say? As soon as the rebels hear of it, they will come and kill us.'

'I have done what is right,' replied Lala very quietly. 'I have not given shelter to *Angrezans*. I have given shelter to friends. Let people say or think as they please.'

He seldom went out of the house, and was usually to be seen seated before the front door, either smoking his small hookah, or playing chess with some friend who happened to drop by. After a few days, people began to suspect that there was somebody in the house about whom Lala was being very discreet, but they had no idea who these guests could be. He kept a close watch on his family, to prevent them from talking too much; and he saw that no one entered the house, keeping the front door chained at all times.

It is a wonder that we were able to live undiscovered for as long as we did, for there were always the dogs to draw attention to the house. They would not leave us, though we had nothing to offer them except the leftovers from our own meals. Lala's aunt told Mother that the third of our dogs, who had not followed us, had been seen going round and round the smoking ruins of our bungalow, and that on the day after the outbreak, he was found dead, sitting up—waiting for his master's return!

* * * * * *

One day, Lala came in while we were seated on the floor talking about recent events. Anxiety for the morrow had taken the edge off our grief, and we were able to speak of what had happened without becoming hysterical.

Lala sat down on the ground with a foil in his hand—the weapon had become his inseparable companion, but I do not think he had yet had occasion to use it. It was not his own, but one that he had found on the floor of the looted and ransacked courthouse.

'Do you think we are safe in your house, Lala? asked Mother. 'What is going on outside these days?'

'You are quite safe here,' said Lala, gesturing with the foil. 'No one comes into this house except over my dead body. It is true, though, that I am suspected of harbouring *kafirs*. More than one person has asked me why I keep such a close watch over my house. My reply is that as the outbreak has put me out of employment, what would they have me do except sit in front of my house and look after my women? Then they ask me why I have not been to the Nawab, like everyone else.'

'What Nawab, Lala?' asked Mother.

'After the sepoys entered the city, their leader, the Subedar-Major, set up Qadar Ali Khan as the Nawab, and proclaimed it throughout the city. Nizam Ali, a pensioner, was made Kotwal, and responsible posts were offered to Javed Khan and to Nizam Ali Khan, but the latter refused to accept office.'

'And the former?'

'He has taken no office yet, because he and Azzu Khan have been too busy plundering the sahibs' houses. Javed Khan also instigated an attack on the treasurer. It was like this . . .

'Javed Khan, as you know, is one of the biggest ruffians in the city. When the sepoys had returned to their lines after proclaiming the Nawab, Javed Khan paid a visit to their commander. On learning that the regiment was preparing to leave Shahjahanpur and join the Bareilly brigade, he persuaded the Subedar-Major, Ghansham Singh, to make a raid on the Rosa Rum Factory before leaving*. A detachment, under Subedar Zorawar Singh, accompanied Javed Khan, and they took the road which passes by Jhunna Lal, the treasurer's house. There they halted, and demanded a contribution from Jhunna Lal. It so happened that he had only that morning received a sum of six thousand rupees from the Tehsildar of Jalalabad, and this the Subedar seized at once. As Jhunna Lal refused to part with any more, he was tied hand and foot and suspended from a tree by his legs. At the same time Javed Khan seized all his account books and threw them into a well, saying, "Since you won't give us what we need, there go your accounts! We won't leave you with the means of collecting money from others!"

'After the party had moved on, Jhunna Lal's servants took him down from the tree. He was half-dead with fright, and from the rush of blood to his head. But when he came to himself, he got his servants to go down the well and fish up every account book!'

'And what about the Rosa Factory?' I asked.

'Javed Khan's party set fire to it, and no less than 70,000 gallons of rum, together with a large quantity of loaf sugar, were destroyed. The rest was carried

---

* *The Rosa Rum Factory survives to this day.*

away. Javed Khan's share of loaf sugar was an entire cartload!'

* * * * * *

The next day when Lala came in and sat beside us—he used to spend at least an hour in our company every day—I asked him a question that had been on my mind much of the time, but the answer to which I was afraid of hearing: the whereabouts of my father's body.

'I would have told you before, *missy-baba,*' he said, 'but I was afraid of upsetting you. The day after I brought you to my house I went again to the church, and there I found the body of your father, of the Collector-Sahib, and the doctor, exactly where I had seen them the day before. In spite of their exposure and the great heat they had not decomposed at all, and neither the vultures nor the jackals had touched them. Only their shoes had gone.

'As I turned to leave I saw two persons, Muslims, bringing in the body of Captain James, who had been shot at a little distance from the church. They laid it beside that of your father and Dr Bowling. They told me that they had decided to bury the mortal remains of those Christians who had been killed. I told them that they were taking a risk in doing so, as they might be accused by the Nawab's men of being in sympathy with the *Firangis.* They replied that they were aware of the risk, but that something had impelled them to undertake this task, and that they were willing to face the consequences.

'I was put to shame by their intentions, and, removing my long coat, began to help them carry the bodies to a pit they had dug outside the church. Here I saw, and was able to identify, the bodies of Mr MacCullam, the *Padri*-Sahib, and Mr Smith, the Assistant Collector. All six were buried side-by-side, and we covered the grave with a masonry slab upon which we drew parallel lines to mark each separate grave. We finished the work within an hour, and when I left the place I felt a satisfaction which I cannot describe . . .'

* * * * * *

Later, when we had recovered from the emotions which Ramjimal's words had aroused in us, I asked him how Mr MacCullam, the chaplain, had met his death; for I remembered seeing him descending from his pulpit when the ruffians entered the church, and running through the vestry with Mr Ricketts' mother.

'I cannot tell you much,' said Lala. 'I only know that while the sepoys attacked Mr Ricketts, Mr MacCullam was able to reach the melon field and conceal himself under some creepers. But another gang found him there, and finished him off with their swords.'

'Poor Mr MacCullam!' sighed Mother. 'He was such a harmless little man. And what about Arthur Smith, Lala?' Mother was determined to find out what had happened to most of the people we had known.

'Assistant-Sahib was murdered in the city,' said Lala. 'He was in his bungalow, ill with fever, when the trouble broke out. His idea was to avoid the cantonment and make for the city, thinking it was only the sepoys who had mutinied. He went to the courts, but found them a shambles, and while he was standing in the street, a mob collected round him and began to push him about. Somebody prodded him with the hilt of his sword. Mr Smith lost his temper and, in spite of his fever, drew his revolver and shot at the man. But alas for Smith-Sahib, the cap snapped and the charge refused to explode. He levelled again at the man, but this time the bullet had no effect, merely striking the metal clasp of the man's belt and falling harmlessly to the ground. Mr Smith flung away his revolver in disgust, and now the man cut at him with his sword and brought him to his knees. Then the mob set upon him. Fate was against Smith-Sahib. The Company Bahadur's prestige had gone, for who ever heard of a revolver snapping, or a bullet being resisted by a belt?'

A Change of Name

According to the reports we received from Lala Ramjimal, it seemed that by the middle of June every European of Shahjahanpur had been killed—if not in the city, then at Muhamdi, across the Khannaut, where many, including Mrs Bowling and her child, had fled. The only survivors were ourselves and (as we discovered later) the Redmans. And we had survived only because the outer world believed that we, too, had perished. This was made clear to us one day when a woman came to the door to sell fish.

Lala's wife remarked: 'You have come after such a long time. And you don't seem to have sold anything today?'

'Ah, Lalain!' said the woman. 'Who is there to buy from me? The *Firangis* are gone. There was a time when I used to be at the Labadoor house every day, and I never went away without making four or five annas. Not only did the memsahib buy from me, but sometimes she used to get me to cook the fish for her, for which she used to pay me an extra two annas.'

'And what has become of them?' asked Lalain.

'Why, the sahib and his daughter were killed in the church, while the memsahib went and threw herself in the river.'

'Are you sure of this?' asked Lalain.

'Of course!' said the woman. 'My husband, while fishing next morning, saw her body floating down the Khannaut!'

* * * * * *

We had been in Lala Ramjimal's house for two weeks, and our clothes had become dirty and torn. There had been no time to bring any clothing with us, and there was no possibility of changing, unless we adopted Indian dress. And so Mother borrowed a couple of petticoats and light shawls from Lalain, and altered them to our measurements. We had to wash them in the courtyard whenever they became dirty, and stand around wrapped in sheets until they were half-dry.

Mother also considered it prudent to take Indian names. I was given the name of Khurshid, which is Persian for 'sun', and my cousin Anet, being short of stature, was called Nanni. Pilloo was named Ghulam

Husain, and his mother automatically became known as Ghulam Husain's mother. Granny was, of course, Bari-bi. It was easier for us to take Mohammedan names, because we were fluent in Urdu, and because Granny did in fact come from a Muslim family of Rampur. We soon fell into the habits of Lala's household, and it would have been very difficult for anyone, who had known us before, to recognize us as the Labadoors.

Life in Lala's house was not without its touches of humour. There lived with us a woman named Ratna, wife to Imrat Lal, a relative of Lala's. He was a short, stout man. She was tall, and considered ugly. He had no children by her, and after some time, had become intimate with a low-caste woman who used to fill water for his family and was, like himself, short and stout. He had two sons by her, and though his longing for children was now satisfied, his peace of mind was soon disturbed by the wranglings of his two wives. He was an astrologer by profession; and, one day, after consulting the stars, he made up his mind to desert his family and seek his fortune elsewhere. His wives, left to themselves, now made up their differences and began to live together. The first wife earned a living as a seamstress, the second used to grind. Occasionally, there would be outbreaks of jealousy. The second wife would taunt the first for being barren, and the seamstress would reply, 'When you drew water, you had corns on your hands and feet. Now grinding has given you corns on your fingers. Where next are you going to get corns?'

Imrat Lal had, meanwhile, become a yogi and soothsayer and began to make a comfortable living in Haridwar. Having heard of his whereabouts, the second wife had a petition writer draw up a letter for her, which she asked me to read to her, as I knew Urdu. It went something like this:

'O thou who hast vanished like mustard oil which, when absorbed by the skin, leaves only its odour behind; thou with the rotund form dancing before my eyes, and the owl's eyes which were wont to stare at me vacantly; wilt thou still snap thy fingers at me when this letter is evidence of my unceasing thought of thee? Why did you call me your *lado*, your loved one, when you had no love for me? And why have you left me to the taunts of that stick of a woman whom you in your perversity used to call a precious stone, your Ratna? Who has proved untrue, you or I? Why have you sported thus with my feelings? Drown yourself in a handful of water, or return and make my hated rival an ornament for your neck, or wear her effigy nine times round your arm as a charm against my longings for you.'

But she received no reply to this letter. Probably when Imrat Lal read it, he consulted the stars again, and decided it was best to move further on into the hills, leaving his family to the care of his generous relative, Lala Ramjimal.

* * * * * *

As the hot weather was now at its height everyone slept out in the courtyard, including Lala and the female members of his household. We had become one vast family. Everyone slept well, except Mother, who, though she rested during the day, stayed awake all night, watching over us. It was distressing to see her sit up night after night, determined not to fall asleep. Her forebodings of danger were as strong as before. Lala would fold his hands to her and say, 'Do sleep, Mariam. I am no Mathur if I shirk my duty.' But her only reply was to ask him for a knife that she could keep beside her. He gave her a rusty old knife, and she took great pains to clean it and sharpen its edges.

A day came when mother threatened to use it.

It was ten o'clock and everyone had gone to bed, except Mother, who still sat at the foot of my cot. I was just dozing off when she remarked that she could smell jasmine flowers, which was strange, because there was no jasmine bush near the house. At the same time a clod of earth fell from the high wall, and looking up, we saw in the dark the figure of a man stretched across it. There was another man a little further along, concealed in the shadows of a neem tree that grew at the end of the yard. Mother drew her knife from beneath her pillow, and called out that she would pierce the heart of the first man who attempted to lay his hands on us. Impressed by her ferocity, which was like that of a tigress guarding her young, the intruders quietly disappeared into the night.

This incident led us to believe that we were still unsafe, and that our existence was known to others. A few days later something else happened that made us even more nervous.

Lado, one of the two servants who had followed us, had been permitted by Lala to occupy a corner of the house. She had a daughter married to a local sword-cleaner, who had been going about looking for Lado ever since the outbreak. Hearing the rumour that there were *Firangis* hiding in Lala's house, he appeared at the front door on the 23rd of June, and spoke to Lala.

'I am told that my mother-in-law is here,' he said. 'I have enquired everywhere and people tell me that she was seen to come only as far as this. So, Lalaji, you had better let me take her away, or I shall bring trouble upon you.'

Lala denied any knowledge of Lado's whereabouts, but the man was persistent, and asked to be allowed to search the house.

'You will do no such thing,' said Ramjimal. 'Go your way, insolent fellow. How dare you propose to enter my zenana?'

The man left in a huff, threatening to inform the Nawab, and to bring some sepoys to the house. When Lado heard of what had happened, she came into the room and fell at Mother's feet, insisting that she leave immediately, lest her son-in-law brought us any trouble. She blessed me and my cousin, and left the house in tears. Poor Lado! She had been with us many years, and we had all come to like her. She had touched our hearts with her loyalty during our troubles.

In the evening, when Lala came home, he told us of what had befallen Lado. She had met her son-in-law in the city.

'Where have you been Mother?' he had said. 'I have been searching for you everywhere. From where have you suddenly sprung up?'

'I am just returning from Fatehgarh,' she said.

'Why, Mother, what took you to Fatehgarh? And what has become of the *Angrezans* you were serving?'

'Now how am I to know what became of them?' replied Lado. 'They were all killed, I suppose. Someone saw Labadoor-Mem drowned in the Khannaut.'

The Nawab heard of the sudden reappearance of our old servant. He sent for her and had her closely questioned; but Lado maintained that she did not know what had happened to us.

The Nawab swore at her. 'This "dead one" tries to bandy words with me,' he said. 'She knows where they are, but will not tell. On my oath, I will have your head chopped off, unless you tell me everything you know about them. Do you hear?'

'My Lord!' answered Lado, trembling from head to foot, 'how can I tell you what I do not know myself? True, I fled with them from the burning house, but where they went afterwards, I do not know.'

'This she-devil!' swore the Nawab. 'She will be the cause of my committing a violent act. She evades the truth. All right, let her be dealt with according to her desserts.'

Two men rushed up, and, seizing Lado by the hair, held a naked sword across her throat. The poor woman writhed and wriggled in the grasp of her captors, protesting her innocence and begging for mercy.

'I swear by your head, My Lord, that I know nothing.'

'So you swear by my head, too?' raged the Nawab. 'Well, since you are not afraid even of the sword, I suppose you know nothing. Let her go.'

And poor Lado, half-dead through fright, was released and sent on her way.

Another Nawab

On the 24th of June there was a great beating of drums, and in the distance we heard the sound of fife and drum. We hadn't heard these familiar sounds since the day of the outbreak, and now we wondered what could be happening. There was much shouting on the road, and the trample of horses, and we waited impatiently for Lala to come home and satisfy our curiosity.

'A change of Nawabs today?' enquired Mother. 'How will it affect us?'

'It isn't possible to say as yet. Ghulam Qadar Khan is the same sort of man as his predecessor, and they come from the same family. Both of them were opposed to the Company's rule. There is this difference, though: whereas Qadar Ali was a dissolute character and ineffective in many ways, Ghulam Qadar has energy, and is said to be pious—but he, too, has expressed his determination to rid this land of all *Firangis* . . .

'When the Mutiny first broke out, he was in Oudh, where he had been inciting the rural population to throw off the foreign yoke. He would have acted in unison with Qadar Ali had they not already disagreed; for Ghulam Qadar was against the murder of women and children. However, Qadar Ali's counsels prevailed, and Ghulam Qadar withdrew for a while, to watch the course of events. Now several powerful landholders have thrown their lot in with him, including Nizam Ali Khan, Vittal Singh, Abdul Rauf, and even that ruffian, Javed Khan. Yesterday he entered Shahjahanpur and without any opposition took over the government. This morning the leading rebels attended the durbar of the new Nawab. And tonight the Nawab holds an entertainment.'

'Do you think he will trouble us, Lala?' asked Granny anxiously. 'What has he to gain by killing such harmless people as us?'

'I cannot say anything for certain, Bari-Bi,' said Lala. 'He might wish to popularize, his reign by exterminating a few *kafirs* as his predecessor did. But there is a rumour in the city that he has been afflicted with some deep sorrow . . .'

'What could it be?' asked Mother. 'Is his wife dead? Surely he can get another, especially now that he is the Nawab. And how can his grief affect us?'

'It could influence his actions,' said Lala. 'The rumour is that his daughter Zinat, a young and beautiful girl, has been abducted by a lover. Where she has been taken, no one knows.'

'And the lover?' asked Mother, displaying for a moment her habitual curiosity about other people's romantic affairs.

'They say that Farhat, one of Qadar Ali's sons, disappeared at the same time. They suspect that he has eloped with the girl.'

'Ah, I remember Farhat,' said Mother. 'A handsome young fellow who often passed in front of our house, showing off on a piebald nag. Still, what has all this to do with us?'

'I was coming to that, Mariam,' said Lala. 'No sooner had the Nawab taken his seat at the durbar, than some informers came to him with the story about Lado, and suggested that my house be searched for your family. Well, the Nawab wanted to know what had happened to Labadoor-Sahib who, he remarked, had always been a harmless and inoffensive man. When told that he had been killed along with the others in the church, the Nawab said, "So be it. Then we need not go out of our way to look for his women. I will have nothing to do with the murder of the innocent . . ."'

'How far can we trust his present mood?' asked Mother.

'I was told by Nizam Ali Khan that the Nawab once gave his daughter a certain promise—that he would not lift his hand against the women and children of the *Firangis*. It sounds very unlikely, I know. But I think Nizam Ali's information is usually reliable.'

'That is true,' said Mother. 'My husband knew him well. We had the lease of his compound for several years, and we paid the rent regularly.'

'Well, the Nawab likes him,' said Lala. 'He has given him orders to begin casting guns in his private armoury. If the Nawab sticks to men like Nizam Ali, public affairs will be handled more efficiently than they would have been under Qadar Ali Khan.'

* * * * * *

We had all along been dependent upon Lala Ramjimal for our daily necessities and though Mother had a little money in her jewel box, which she had brought with her, she had to use it very sparingly.

One day, folding his hands before her, Lala said, 'Mariam, I am ashamed to say it, but I have no money left. Business has been at a standstill, and the little money I had saved is all but finished.'

'Don't be upset, Lala,' said Mother, taking some leaf-gold from her jewel box and giving it to him. 'Take this gold to the bazaar, and sell it for whatever you can get.'

Lala was touched, and at the same time overjoyed at this unexpected help.

'I shall go to the bazaar immediately and see what I can get for it,' he said. 'And I have a suggestion, Mariam. Let us all go to Bareilly. I have my brother there, and some of your relatives are also there. We shall at least save on house rent, which I am paying here. If you agree, I will hire two carts which should accommodate all of us.'

We readily agreed to Lala's suggestion, and he walked off happily to the bazaar, unaware that his plans for our safety were shortly to go awry.

Caught!

We had been with Lala almost a month, and this was to be our last day in his house.

We were, as usual, huddled together in one room, discussing our future prospects, when our attention was drawn to the sound of men's voices outside.

'Open the door!' shouted someone, and there was a loud banging on the front door.

We did not answer the summons, but cast nervous glances at each other. Lalain, who had been sitting with us, got up and left the room, and chained our door from the other side.

'Open up or we'll force your door in!' demanded the voice outside, and the banging now became more violent.

Finally, Ratna went to the front door and opened it, letting in some twenty to thirty men, all armed with swords and pistols. One of them, who had done all the shouting and seemed to be the leader, ordered the women to go up to the roof of the house, as he intended searching all the rooms for the fugitive *Firangis*. Lala's family had no alternative but to obey him, and they went up to the roof. The men now approached the door of our room, and we heard the wrench of the chain as it was drawn out. The leader, pushing the door open violently, entered the room with a naked sword in his hand.

'Where is Labadoor's daughter?' he demanded of Mother, gripping her by the arm and looking intently into her face. 'No, this is not her,' he said, dropping her hand and turning to look at me.

'This is the girl!' he exclaimed, taking me by the hand and dragging me away from Mother into the light of the courtyard. He held his uplifted sword in his right hand.

'No!' cried Mother in a tone of anguish, throwing herself in front of me. 'If you would take my daughter's life, take mine before hers, I beg of you by the sword of Ali!'

Her eyes were bloodshot, starting out of their sockets, and she presented a magnificent, and quite terrifying sight. I think she frightened me even more than the man with the raised sword; but I clung to her instinctively, and tried to wrest my arm from the man's grasp. But so impressed was he by Mother's display that he dropped the point of his sword and in a gruff voice commanded us both to follow him quietly if we valued our lives. Granny sat wringing her hands in desperation, while the others remained huddled together in a corner, concealing Pilloo, the only boy, beneath their shawls. The man with the sword led Mother and me from the house, followed by his band of henchmen.

* * * * * *

It was the end of June, and the monsoon rains had not yet arrived. It was getting on for noon, and the sun beat down mercilessly. The ground was hard and dry and dusty. Barefooted and bareheaded, we followed our captor without a murmur, like lambs going to slaughter. The others hemmed us in, all with drawn swords, their steel blades glistening in the sun. We had no idea where we were being taken, or what was in store for us.

After walking half a mile, during which our feet were blistered on the hot surface of the road, our captor halted under a tamarind tree, near a small mosque, and told us to rest. We told him we were thirsty, and some water was brought to us in a brass jug. A crowd of curious people had gathered around us.

'These are the *Firangans* who were hiding with the Lala! How miserable they look. But one is young—she has fine eyes! They are her mother's eyes—notice!'

A pir, a wandering hermit, who was in the group, touched our captor on the shoulder and said, 'Javed, you have taken away these unfortunates to amuse yourself. Give me your word of honour that you will not ill-treat or kill them.'

'So this is Javed Khan,' whispered Mother.

Javed Khan, his face still muffled, brought his sword to a slant before his face. 'I swear by my sword that I will neither kill nor ill-treat them!'

'Take care for your soul, Javed,' said the pir. 'You have taken an oath which no Pathan would break and still expect to survive. Let no harm come to these two, or you may expect a short lease of life!'

'Have no fear for that!' said Javed Khan, signalling us to rise.

We followed him as before, leaving, the crowd of gazers behind, and taking the road that led into the narrow mohalla of Jalalnagar, the Pathan quarter of the city.

Passing down several lanes, we arrived at a small square, at one end of which a horse was tied. Javed Khan slapped the horse on the rump, and opening the door of his house, told us to enter. He came in behind us. In the courtyard, we saw a young woman sitting on a swing. She seemed astonished to see us.

'These are the *Firangans*,' said Javed Khan, closing the front door behind him and walking unconcernedly across the courtyard.

An elderly woman approached Mother.

'Don't be afraid,' she said. 'Sit down and rest a little.'

Javed Khan

When Javed Khan returned to his zenana after a wash and a change of clothes, he addressed his wife.

'What do you think of my *Firangans*? Didn't I say I would not rest until I found them? A lesser man would have given up the search long ago!' And chuckling, he sat down to his breakfast, which was served to him on a low, wooden platform.

His aunt, the elderly woman who had first welcomed us, and who was known as Kothiwali, spoke gently to Mother.

'Tell me,' she said, 'tell me something of your story. Who are you?'

'You see us for what we are,' replied Mother. 'Dependent on others, at the mercy of your relative who may kill us whenever it takes his fancy.'

'Who is going to take your miserable lives?' interrupted Javed Khan.

'No, you are safe while I am here,' said Kothiwali. 'You may speak to me without fear. What is your name, and that of the girl with you?'

'The girl is Khurshid, my only daughter. My name is Mariam, and my family is well-known in Rampur, where my father was a minister to the Nawab.'

'Which Rampur?' asked Khan-Begum, Javed's wife.

'*Rohelon-ka-Rampur*,' replied Mother.

'Oh, *that* Rampur!' said Khan-Begum, evidently impressed by Mother's antecedents.

'This, my only child,' continued Mother bestowing an affectionate glance at me, 'is the offspring of an Englishman. He was massacred in the church, on the day the outbreak took place. So I am now a widow, and the child, fatherless. Our lives were saved through the kindness of Lala Ramjimal, and we were living at his house until your relative took us away by force. My mother and others of our family are still there. Only Allah knows what will become of us all, for there is no one left to protect us.'

Mother's feelings now overcame her, and she began weeping. This set me off too, and hiding my face in Mother's shawl, I began to sob.

Kothiwali was touched. She place her hand on my head and said, 'Don't weep, child, don't weep,' in a sympathetic tone.

Mother wiped the tears from her eyes and looked up at the older woman. 'We are in great trouble, Pathani!' she said. 'Spare our lives and don't let us be dishonoured, I beg of you.'

Javed Khan, quite put out by all this weeping, now exclaimed, 'Put your mind at rest, good woman. No one will kill you, I can assure you. On the contrary, I have saved your daughter from dishonour at the hands of others. I intend to marry her honourably, whenever you will.'

* * * * * *

The plate dropped from Javed Khan's wife's hand. He gave her a fierce look. 'Don't be such a fool, Qabil!' he said.

Before Mother could say anything, Kothiwali said, 'Javed, you should not have done this thing. These two are of good birth, and they are in distress. Look how faded and careworn they are! Be kind to them, I tell you, and do not insult them in their present condition.'

'Depend on it, Chachi,' he replied. 'They will receive nothing but kindness from my hands. True, now they have fallen from their former greatness!'

'I should like to know how you became acquainted with them?' enquired Kothiwali. 'Is not your Khan-Begum as good a wife as any? Mark her fine nose!'

'Who says anything to the contrary? But, oh Chachi!' he exclaimed. 'How can I make you understand the fascination this girl exerted over me when she was in her father's house! The very first time I saw her, I was struck by her beauty. She shone like Zohra, the morning star. Looking at her now, I realize the truth of the saying that a flower never looks so beautiful as when it is on its parent stem. Break it, and it withers in the hand. Would anyone believe that this poor creature is the same angelic one I saw only a month ago?'

I was full of resentment, but could say nothing and do nothing, except press closer to my mother and look at Javed Khan with all the scorn I could muster. Khan-Begum, too, must have been seething with indignation; but she too was helpless, because Javed was well within his rights to think in terms of a second wife.

'The greater fool you, Javed, for depriving the child of her father, and breaking the flower from its stem before it had bloomed!' said Khan-Begum.

'What did you say, Qabil?' he asked sharply. 'No, don't repeat it again. The demon is only slumbering in my breast, and it will take little to rouse it.'

He gave me a scorching look, and I could not take my eyes from his face; I was like a doomed bird, fascinated by the gaze of a rattlesnake. But Mother was staring at him as though she would plumb his dark soul to its innermost depths, and he quailed under her stern gaze.

'Don't put me down for a common murderer,' he said apologetically. 'If I have taken lives, they have been those of infidels, enemies of my people. I am deserving of praise rather than blame.'

'Now don't excite yourself,' said Kothiwali, coming to the rescue again. 'What I wanted to bring home to you is that if you are such an admirer of beauty, your Khan-Begum is neither ugly nor dark. I should have thought *Firangi* women had blue eyes and fair hair, but these poor things—how frightened they look!—would pass off as one of us!'

'All right, all right,' grumbled Javed Khan in a harsh voice. 'Don't carry on and on about Qabil's beauty, as if she ever possessed any. Let us drop the subject. But Chachi,' and his eyes softened as he glanced at me, 'you should have judged this girl at the time I first set eyes on her. She was like a rose touched by a breath of wind, a doe-like creature . . .'

'Will you not stop your rubbish?' interrupted Kothiwali. 'Look at her now, and tell me if she answers the same description.'

'*W'allah!* A change has come over them!' exclaimed Javed Khan wonderingly, becoming poetical again. 'She is not what she used to be. Within a month she has aged twenty years. When I seized the girl by her arm at the Lala's house, she was ready to faint. But oh, how can I describe the terror which seized me at the sight of her mother! Like an enraged tigress, whose side has been pierced by a barbed arrow, she hurled herself at me and presented her breast to my sword. I shall never forget the look she gave me as she thrust me away from the girl! I was awed. I was subdued. I was unmanned. The sword was ready to fall from my hand. Surely the blood of a hero runs in her veins! This is no ordinary female!' And bestowing a kindly glance on Mother, he exclaimed: 'A hundred mercies to thee, woman!'

Guests of the Pathan

'I think you and I will be good friends,' said Kothiwali to Mother. 'I already love your daughter. Come, *beti*, come nearer to me,' she said, caressing my head.

Javed Khan had finished his meal and had gone out into the courtyard, leaving his wife and aunt alone to eat with us. Though we were hungry and thirsty, we did not have the heart to eat much with Granny's, and cousin Anet's fate still unknown to us. But we took something, enough to keep up our strength, and when Javed Khan came in again, he seemed pleased that we had partaken of his food.

'Having tasted salt under my roof,' he said, 'you are no longer strangers in the house. You must make my house your home for the future.'

'It is very good of you to say so,' replied Mother. 'But there are others who are dependent on me, my mother and my niece, and without them everything I eat tastes bitter in my mouth.'

'Don't worry, they shall join you,' said Javed Khan. 'I had seen your daughter a long time before the outbreak, when I took a fancy to her. A ruffian had intended to carry her off before and would have done so had I not anticipated him. I have brought you here with the best of intentions. As soon as I have your consent, I propose to marry Khurshid, and will give her a wife's portion.'

'But how can you do that?' asked Mother. 'You have a wife already.'

'Well, what is there to prevent me having more wives than one? Our law allows it.'

'That may be,' rejoined Mother, 'but how can you, a Muslim, marry a Christian girl?'

'There is no reason why I may not,' replied Javed Khan. 'We Pathans can take a wife from any race or creed we please. And—' pausing as his wife let fall a petulant 'Oh!'—'I dare my wife to object to such a proceeding on my part. Did not my father take in a low-caste woman for her large, pretty eyes, the issue of that union being the brat, Saifullah—a plague on him!—and Kothiwali, whom you see here, was a low-caste Hindu who charmed my uncle out of his wits. So what harm can there be if I take a Christian for a wife?'

My mother had a quiver full of counter arguments, but the time was not favourable for argument; it was safer to dissemble.

'I trust you will not expect an immediate answer to your request,' she said. 'I have just lost my husband, and there is no one to guide or advise me. Let us speak again on this subject at some other time.'

'I am in no hurry,' said Javed Khan. 'A matter of such importance cannot be settled in a day. Take a week, good woman. And do not forget that this is no sudden infatuation on my part. The girl has been in my mind for months. I am not Javed if I let the opportunity pass me by. Be easy in your mind—there is no hurry . . .'

And he went out again into the courtyard.

* * * * * *

All that had happened to us that morning, and Javed Khan's proposal of marriage, gave me food for thought for the rest of the day. A bed was put down for us in the veranda, and I lay down on my back, staring up at the ceiling where two small lizards darted about in search of flies. Mother was engrossed in a conversation with Kothiwali. Her perfect Urdu, her fine manners, and her high moral values, all took Kothiwali by storm. She was in raptures over Mother, and expressed every sympathy for us. She had come to Javed's house on a short visit, and did not feel like leaving.

'You must let Mariam come and spend a few days with me,' she said to her niece.

'And what is to become of her daughter?' replied Khan-Begum. 'Is she to be left here alone?'

'Of course not. She must come with her mother. And, Qabil, don't allow all this to upset you. Javed's head is a little befuddled nowadays, but he will be all right soon. As for these poor things, they are in no way to blame. You will come, Mariam, won't you?'

'With pleasure,' said Mother. 'If we are allowed to.'

* * * * * *

We were worrying about Granny and the others when the sound of an altercation at the front door reached us. We recognized the voice of our friend and protector, Lala Ramjimal, who had tracked us down, and now insisted on seeing us.

'Khan Saheb!' we heard him say to Javed Khan. 'It was very wrong of you to enter my house during my absence and bring away my guests without my permission. Had I been there, you could only have done so by making your way over my dead body.'

'That is exactly why I came when you were not there,' replied Javed Khan. 'I had no wish to end your life.'

'I would not be a Mathur if I had not defended them. Well, what is done is done. I cannot force you to return them to my house. But let me be permitted to see if they need anything. I will also say goodbye to them.'

Mother went to the door and spoke to Lala, thanking him for taking the risk in coming to see us.

'What Vishnu ordered has come to pass,' said Lala resignedly. 'No skill of ours could have prevented it. But be comforted, for better days must lie ahead. I have brought your jewel box back for you.'

She took the jewel box from his hand, but did not bother to examine its contents, knowing that nothing would be missing.

'I have sold the gold you gave me,' said Lala, 'and I have brought the price of it—thirty rupees. I shall bring Bari-Bi and Nani to you this evening. The others can stay with me a little longer.'

'Oh, Lala!' said Mother. 'How are we to repay you for all your kindness?'

'I shall be repaid in time to come.' said Lala. 'But what is to become of your dogs?'

'Keep them, Lala, or do what you like with them. It is going to be difficult enough for us to look after ourselves.'

'True,' he said. 'I shall take them with me to Bareilly and keep them for you.'

He made a low bow to Mother and left us, and that was the last we saw of him.

* * * * * *

We heard later that Lala had taken his family to Bareilly, along with our old servant, Dhani. We never knew what became of the dogs. That evening, Javed Khan had himself gone to Lala's house and brought away Granny and Anet, who were overjoyed to see us. According to the laws of hospitality, food was immediately put before them.

Our party of eight had now been thinned to four. Pilloo and his mother, and Champa, had been left at Lala's house, and we were not to know what became of them until some time afterwards. Javed Khan did not fancy introducing into his household a *Firangi* boy of fourteen. It was fortunate for Pilloo that he was left behind, otherwise he would surely have been killed by one of the cutthroats who lived in the mohalla near Javed's house.

Pilloo's Fate

In order to preserve some sort of sequence, I must record what happened to the three members of our household who were left at Lala's house.

No sooner had he and Javed Khan left the house with Granny and cousin Anet, than it was beset again by another band of Pathans, headed by one Mangal Khan. He forced his way into the house, the Lala's womenfolk retired to the roof as before, and Pilloo, his mother, and Champa, their servant, shut themselves in their room.

'Where is the *Firangi* youth?' shouted Mangal Khan. 'Bring him out, so that we may deal with him as we have dealt with others of his kind.'

Seeing that there was no means of escape, Pilloo's mother came out, and falling at Mangal Khan's feet, begged him to spare her son's life.

'*Your* son!' he said, eyeing her disbelievingly from head to foot, for she had a swarthy complexion. 'Let's see what sort of fellow he is.'

Pilloo now came out dressed fantastically, a perfect caricature of a Kayastha boy—pantaloons and shirt; no socks or shoes or headdress—all but his face and fair complexion, which could not be disguised.

'This fellow does not even reach my shoulders,' said Mangal Khan, standing over him. 'How old are you?' he asked sternly.

Pilloo was trembling all over with fright and was unable to answer; instead, he looked at his mother.

She folded her hands and replied, 'Your slave is not more than fourteen, Khan Saheb! I beg of you, spare his life for the Prophet's sake! Do what you like with me, but spare the boy.' And Pilloo's mother rained tears, and fell at his feet again.

The Pathan was moved by these repeated appeals to his feelings.

'Get up, woman!' he said. 'I can see the boy is young and harmless. Will both of you come with me? Remember, if you don't, there are others who will not be as soft-hearted as I.'

Lala's house was obviously no longer safe as a hiding-place, and Pilloo's mother agreed to accompany Mangal Khan. So off they were marched, together with Champa, to another mohalla inhabited chiefly by Pathans, where they were hospitably received at Mangal Khan's house.

Mangal Khan was at heart a generous man. After he had taken the fugitives under his roof, he showed them every kindness and consideration. He called Pilloo by his new name, Ghulam Husain, and his mother continued to be known as Ghulam Husain's mother. Champa, of course, remained Champa. She was a Rajput girl, and there was no mistaking her for anything else.

Pilloo and his mother continued to live under the protection of Mangal Khan. What their subsequent fortunes were we did not know until much later, many months after we had left Lala Ramjimal's house.

Further Alarms

It was in our interests to forget that we had European blood in our veins, and that there was any advantage in the return of the British to power. It was also necessary for us to *seem* to forget that the Christian God was our God, and we allowed it to be believed that we were Muslims. Kothiwali often offered to teach us the *Kalma,* but Mother would reply that she knew it already, which was perfectly true. When she was asked to attend prayers with the others, her excuse would be: 'How can we? Our clothes are unclean and we have no others.'

The only clothes we had were those acquired in Lala Ramjimal's house, and, on our third day in Javed's house, he seemed to notice them for the first time.

'Mariam,' he said. 'It won't do to wear such clothes in my house. You must get into a pyjama.'

'Where have I the means to make pyjamas?' asked Mother.

And the same day Javed went and bought some black chintz in the bazaar, and handed it over to Mother. She made us pyjamas and kurta-dupattas, cutting the material, while Anet and I did the sewing. Khan-Begum was astonished to find that Mother could cut so well, and that Anet and I were so adept with our needles.

Before we changed into our new clothes, Mother suggested that we be given facilities for bathing. I think we had not bathed for a month, for in Lala's house there was no water close at hand; his women folk would bathe every morning at the river, but it had been too dangerous for us to go out.

There was a well right in the middle of the courtyard of Javed Khan's house, and so it was quite possible for us to take a cold bath. Mother told Zeban, the female barber of the house, to draw water for us and help us bathe, and that she would reward this service with a payment of four pice—a pice per person—and Zeban was overjoyed at the prospect of this little windfall. She set up a couple of beds at right angles to one another in the courtyard, covering them with sheets to form a screen. Kothiwali had heard that we were going to change our clothes and bathe, and this being quite an event, she arrived at the house in a great fluster, determined to assist us in the mysteries of the bath.

It was the 2nd of July, a day memorable in our lives from a hygienic point of view.

Kothiwali offered to pour water over us with her own hands. To this, however, Mother strenuously objected. She point out that it was not customary among her people to be seen undressed by others, even by members of the same sex, and that she would not therefore, give Kothiwali the trouble.

Kothiwali was dismayed. 'But how can you take the sacred bath and be purified,' she urged, 'unless at least three tumblers of sanctified water are poured on you?'

Mother was ready with her reply. She said that each of us knew the *Kalma*, and that doubtless we would remember the last three tumblers when we came to them. And this embarrassment being overcome, we had the satisfaction of washing our bodies with fresh water from the well, and afterwards, putting on our new clothes, which fitted us perfectly.

After this, we opened our hair to dry, and instantly there were loud exclamations of admiration from the women who were present. Such lovely long hair! And looking at my curls—my hair was not very long but quite wavy—exclaimed at my pretty '*ghungarwala*'. Mother and Granny did indeed have beautiful heads of hair. Granny's reached down to her heels; Mother's, to a little below the knees. Anet's hair, like mine, reached only to the waist, but it was very bushy, and when made into a plait, was as a fat woman's arm. As we sat about drying our hair, the women gazed at us with their mouths open. We explained that the family from which my mother came was distinguished for the long and bushy hair of its females.

We were also faced with the problem of oiling so much hair, and Khan-Begum asked us what oil we used. Mother said we used coconut oil, but no one knew where so much coconut oil could be had. So Khan-Begum gave a pice to Zeban, and had her fetch us some sweet oil from the bazaar. She also sent for a small fine-tooth comb made of horn. Granny got up and oiled and combed Mother's hair, while Mother dressed mine and Anet's, as well as Granny's.

******

Next morning we felt buoyant and refreshed. We busied ourselves in sewing a second suit of clothes, which we intended trying on after taking another bath the following Friday, the day of the week on which most Pathan women bathe.

At ten o'clock, Javed Khan received a visitor in the person of Sarfaraz Khan, his wife's brother-in-law. This man had been a constable in the police service, and had retired to his home on the outbreak of the Mutiny. In accordance with the costume of the time, he was armed with sword, pistol, knife and a double-barrelled gun. He appeared excited as he met Javed Khan at the door.

'You have brought some *Firangans* into the house, Javed?' he said. 'Wouldn't you like to show them to me?'

'You shall see them,' replied Javed, 'and be given the opportunity of appreciating my taste for the beautiful.'

With his hand on his pistol and a menacing look on his bearded face, Sarfaraz Khan strode into the veranda. Khan-Begum stood up and made him a salaam, and we did the same. He sat down on a cot, resting the butt of his gun on the ground, while with one hand he held the barrel—a typical Pathan attitude.

'So these are the *Firangans* who have made such a stir in the mohalla!' he observed.

Javed Khan had gone into the house, and Mother spoke up for us.

'What stir can we make?' she said. 'We are poor, helpless people.'

'And yet everyone is saying that you have come into this house to find a husband for your daughter, and that Javed Khan is going to marry her! Why have you brought trouble to this good woman?' he said, pointing towards Khan-Begum.

Though Mother was indignant at the insinuation, she restrained her feelings, and answered him quietly.

'What are you saying, brother? Surely you know that we would not have entered this house unless we had been compelled to. Javed Khan brought us here by force, from a house where we had received every kindness, in order to please himself. We are grateful for his hospitality, but as to marrying my daughter to him or to anyone else, that is a matter which I am not in a position to discuss, and we are grateful to your brother for not forcing us to agree to his wishes.'

'And yet it is the talk of the mohalla,' said Sarfaraz Khan, 'that Javed intends marrying your daughter, and this talk has put Khan-Begum in a great state of mind!'

'In what way are we responsible for what people say?' replied Mother. 'We would do anything to save Khan-Begum from unhappiness.'

Javed, who had overheard much of the conversation, now stamped in, looking quite ruffled.

'Brother, what is your motive in questioning this good woman and treating these people as though they were intruders? By my head, they are in no way to blame! It was I who brought them to my house, and only I am answerable for their actions.'

'Why have you brought trouble to your good wife?' asked Sarfaraz Khan. 'You have spoilt the good name of our family by your foolish conduct.'

'I know who has sent you here,' remarked Javed, folding his arms across his chest.

'Yes, Abdul Rauf has sent me here to take the women to the riverside, and there strike their heads off, in order that the fire raging in your wife's bosom may be quenched.'

'No one has the right to tell me what I should do in my own house,' said Javed fiercely, drawing himself up to his full height and towering over Sarfaraz Khan. 'If Abdul Rauf is wise, he will look to his own house and family, instead of prying into other people's affairs. I will have none of his interference. As to Qabil, she is a fool for talking too much to the neighbours. I shall have to restrict her liberty.'

The two enraged Pathans would have come to blows, or worse, had not Mother put herself forward again.

'As to cutting off our heads,' she said, 'you have the power Khan Saheb, and we cannot resist. If it should be Allah's will that we die by your hand, let it be so. There is but one favour, however, that I would ask of you, and that is that you kill every one of us, without exception. I shall not allow you to kill one or two only!'

Sarfaraz Khan was touched, both by Mother's courage, and because she had spoken in the name of Allah. He warmed towards her, as others had done.

'Great is your faith, and great your spirit,' he said. 'Well, I wash my hands off this business. To have been sent on a fool's errand, and to be put off by the calm persuasiveness of a woman!'

'It was Allah's will,' said Javed. 'You will not be so foolish again. Why poison your heart on behalf of your relatives? It was their doing, I knew that all along.'

Another Proposal

Two or three days after the visit of Sarfaraz Khan, when we had taken our evening meal, Javed Khan entered the room and made himself comfortable on the low, wooden platform.

'Mariam, you promised to speak to me again on a certain subject which you know is close to my heart,' he said, addressing Mother. 'Now that you have had time to think it over, perhaps you can give me a definite answer.'

'What subject do you mean?' asked Mother, feigning ignorance.

'I mean my original proposal to marry your daughter.'

'I have hardly had time to argue the matter with myself,' said Mother, 'or to give it the attention it deserves. It was only the other day that your brother-in-law came here to kill us without a moment's notice. If we are likely to be killed even while under your protection, what use is there in discussing the subject of marriage? If I am to lose my life, my daughter's life must go too. She and I are inseparable. Someone like Sarfaraz may be on his way here even now!'

'Upon my head, you make me angry when you talk like that!' exclaimed Javed. 'I tell you that had he lifted his hand against either of you, he would have lost his own life. As long as you are under Javed's roof, there is not a man who would dare to raise his finger against you. I shall strike off the heads of half a dozen before a hair on my *Firangan's* head can be touched.' And he gave me a look of such passion and ferocity, that I trembled with fright, and hid my face behind Mother's back.

He was terribly excited, and to calm him mother said, 'I am sure you are strong enough to protect us. But why do you bring up this subject again?'

'Because it is always on my mind. Why delay it any longer?'

'If you knew our circumstances and the history of my family,' said Mother, 'you would see that I am not in a position to give her away.'

'Why so?' asked Javed.

'I have my brothers living. What shall I answer them when they find out that I have given you my daughter in marriage, and the girl is still only a child? And moreover, my husband's younger brother is still alive. I have to consult them before I can decide anything.'

'That may be so,' said Javed. 'But they are not likely to question you, as in all probability they have been killed along with the other *Firangis.*'

'I hope not. But would it not be wiser to wait and make certain they are dead before we come to any definite decision?'

'I am an impatient man, Mariam, and life is not so long that I can wait an eternity to quench my desires. I have restrained myself out of respect for your wishes, and out of respect for you. But my desire to call your girl my wife grows stronger daily, and I am prepared to take any risk to have her for my own.'

'Suppose the English Government is restored to power—what shall we do then? Your life will be worth little, and with you dead, my daughter will be a widow at thirteen. Cannot you wait a few months, until we are certain as to who will remain master of this country?'

'True, if the English retook Shahjahanpur, they would show little mercy to the leaders of the revolt. They would hang me from the nearest tree. And no doubt you are hoping for their return, or you would not talk of such a possibility. But how many of them are left? Only a few thousand struggling to hold their own before the walls of Delhi, and they too will soon be disposed of, please God!'

'Then let Delhi decide our future,' said Mother, seizing at a straw. 'If the British army now besieging

Delhi is destroyed, that will be the time to talk of such matters. Meanwhile, are we not your dependents and in your power? You have only to await the outcome of the war.'

'You point a long way off, Mariam, and seem to forget that I have the power to marry her against your will and the will of everyone else, including'—and he gave his wife a defiant look—'the owner of a pair of jealous eyes now gazing at me!'

'Did I say you did not have that power?' asked Mother. 'If you take her by force, we have no power to resist. But if you were to wait until the British are driven from Delhi, my argument would no longer carry any weight. And by that time, my daughter would be more of an age for marriage.'

'It is fortunate for you that I am a man. No one shall take her away from Javed, and Javed's wife she shall be, and I will give her a handsome dowry. And if you were to take my advice, Mariam, you ought to take a husband as well and settle down again in life. You are still young.'

'Why would I marry now?'

'You should marry, if it be only to find a home of your own and bread with it.'

'Why would I marry?' asked Mother again. 'What would become of my girls?'

'Why, your daughter shall be mine,' said Javed brightly. 'And as to your niece, she too will fit in somewhere! She is not unattractive, you know!'

******

We did not speak much for the rest of the evening. Javed Khan settled himself before a hookah, puffing contentedly, blissfully unaware of the agitation he had set up in everyone's minds. No one spoke. Khan-Begum went about with a long face, and sighed whenever she looked at me. Mother, too, sighed when she looked at me, and Anet and I stared at each other in bewilderment.

As we rose to go to our part of the house, Khan-Begum seized Mother's hand, and in a choking voice, whispered, 'Mariam, you are my mother. Do not help him to inflict greater torment on me than I have already suffered. Promise me that you won't give your daughter to him.'

Mother replied, 'Bibi, you have seen and heard everything that has happened. I am truly a dead one in the hands of the living. You distress yourself for nothing. If I have my way, he shall never get my consent. But will he wait for my consent?'

'Allah bless you!' exclaimed Khan-Begum. 'Your daughter deserves a better fate than to play second fiddle in this family. I will pray that your wishes are granted.'

* * * * * *

I could not sleep much that night. The light from the full moon came through the high, barred window, and fell across the foot of the bed. I dozed a little, but the insistent call of the brain-fever bird kept waking me. I opened my eyes once, and saw Javed Khan standing in the doorway, the moonlight shining on his face. He stood there a long while, staring at me, and I was too afraid to move or call out. Then he turned and walked quietly away; and shivering with fright, I put my arms around Mother, and lay clinging to her for the remainder of the night.

On Show

When Khan-Begum had last visited her husband's sister, the latter had made her promise to come again soon; and on a Thursday, a servant came to her with a message, saying, 'Your sister sends her salaams, and wishes to know when you are going to fulfil your promise of calling on her.'

'Give my respects to my sister,' answered Khan-Begum, 'and tell her I cannot come now. There are some *Firangans* staying with us, brought into the house by my husband.'

Later, another messenger arrived with the suggestion that Khan-Begum take her guests along with her, as her relatives were most anxious to see them too. And so our hostess proposed that we accompany her to her sister Qamran's house the next morning. Four of us set out in one *meana*: Khan-Begum, Mother, Anet and myself. Granny was left behind.

A *meana* is something like a palanquin of old, but smaller, and used exclusively for the conveyance of women. It has short, stubby legs to rest on the ground, the floor is interlaced with string, and the top is covered with red curtains, hanging down the sides. The bearers fix two bamboo poles on either side, by which they lift the *meana* from the ground.

Supported by four perspiring bearers, we arrived at Qamran's house, where we were kindly received. Qamran had at first been prejudiced against us, but the report taken to her by Sarfaraz Khan had made her change her views. She was eager to make our acquaintance and pressed us to stay with her; and during the weeks to come, we were to be her showpieces, on display for those who wanted to see us.

Sarfaraz Khan had come to Javed's house with the intention of striking off our heads, but Mother's charm had baffled him and won him over. Returning home, he had said, 'Who can lift his hand against such harmless things? The girl is like a frightened doe, and the mother—she is a perfect nightingale!' And so, among those who came to see us at Qamran's house was Sarfaraz Khan's wife, Hashmat. She, too, fell a victim to Mother's charm. 'Oh sister!' she exclaimed to Khan-Begum. 'My husband was quite right in his opinion of them. Mariam's lips, like the bee, distil nothing but honey.'

As to Qamran herself, her soft, sympathetic nature was roused by the story of our bereavement and our trails. Her large, pretty black eyes would fill with tears as she listened to Mother, and once she placed her head on Mother's shoulder and sobbed aloud.

She was about thirty-five, and on the verge of becoming stout; but she had fine features and a clear complexion. We were told that when she was dressed for her marriage, her father passed by, and was so struck by her beauty, that he exclaimed: 'Couldn't we have reserved so much beauty for someone who did not have to go out of our family!'

Qamran's husband, a much older man, was a cavalry lieutenant in the army at Bhopal. At their first meeting, she had felt a repugnance for his person. She repelled his advances and would not allow him even to touch her, with the result that her mother and others began to believe that she was in love with a jinn, or spirit. It suited her to encourage them in this belief. Her husband was disgusted, and returned to his cavalry regiment, but continued to keep her supplied with funds. Eventually, through the good offices of mutual friends, they were reconciled, and were blessed with a daughter, whom they named Badran.

Badran's beauty was different from her mother's. At the time we saw her she was sixteen or seventeen; she was slightly darker than her mother, and her eyes, though large, lacked the liquid softness which gave such serenity to Qamran's face. But a pink birthmark on her left cheek gave her an interesting face. She did not have her mother's liveliness or enquiring nature, and we did not see much of her.

* * * * * *

Qamran had heard of our skill with the needle. She had made up her mind to make a present to her sister-in-law's small son, and asked us if we would help make the kurta-topi, which would consist of miniature trousers, coat and cap. Mother offered to cut and sew them.

She gave the kurta, which was of purple cloth, a moghlai neck; that is, it had one opening, buttoning to the side over the left shoulder. It was finished off with gold lace round the edges, the sleeves and the neck. She also gave it a crescent-shaped, gold-embroidered band round the neck, and epaulettes on the shoulders. The trousers were made of rich, green satin, and also finished off with gold lace. The cap was made of the same stuff as the coat, so that it formed a kind of fillet, resting on the forehead. The three garments cost Qamran something like forty rupees—a sumptuous suit for a child!

Mother was pleased with the result of her work, and all who saw the suit were in raptures, and Qamran made Mother a present of a new set of bangles made of glass and enamelled blue.

* * * * * *

We soon established ourselves as favourites in Qamran's house, and members of the household vied with each other in showing us kindness. Whereas they had formely believed that, as *Firangi* women, we would be peeping out of doors and windows in order to be seen by men, without whose society European women were supposed to be unable to live, they were agreeably surprised to find that we delighted in hard work, that we loved needles and thread, and that, far from seeking the company of men, we did our best to avoid them.

'You are like one of us,' said Qamran to Mother one day. 'I would not exchange you for half a dozen women of my own race. Who could possibly ever tire of you?'

Politics seldom entered the four walls of the zenana—wars and deeds of violence were considered the prerogative of men. Seldom was any reference made to the disturbances that were taking place throughout the country, or to our own troubles. Only once was the even tenor of our lives disturbed, and that was due to the woman, Umda, who had taken a jealous dislike to us from the beginning.

I do not know in what way she was related to Qamran, but they addressed each other as 'sister', and Badran called her 'aunt'. She was a spiteful young woman, with a sharp, lashing tongue, very hostile towards all foreign races. She had been very displeased at our introduction into the family, always gave us angry looks, and never missed an opportunity to speak ill of us.

It pleased Umda to hear of the British reverses, and she was convinced that they would be swept from the walls of Delhi. Occasionally, she would leave aside generalities and give her attention to individuals.

Once Mother, Anet and I sat quietly together, sewing a pair of pyjamas for Badran, while Badran herself sat at the end of the veranda, whispering nonsense to her good-natured young husband, Hafizullah Khan. He, however, had his eyes on Umda, for he knew her well.

She began by changing the conversation with a contemptuous reference to the *Firangi* race, bringing up the old story of the hunger of European women for male company.

'Those wantons!' she said. 'They cannot live without the society of men.' 'Perhaps not, Chachi,' observed

Hafizullah Khan from the other end of the veranda, 'and perhaps they are quite right in doing so. They have so much of male company that their appetite for it is probably less than yours. And then not all their men are opium eaters like your husband, who, beyond rolling in the dust like a pig, has little time for anything else.'

'That may be so,' she said haughtily, 'but what has it to do with *Firangi* women? You cannot deny that they enjoy laughing and joking with strange men, that they dance and sing, sometimes half-nude, with the arms of strange men round their waists. Then they retire into dark corners where they kiss and are kissed by men other than their husbands!'

Badran's bright eye had grown wide with astonishment at this recital of the ways of the *Firangi* female.

'I did not know all that,' said Hafizullah Khan. 'From where do you obtain your deep knowledge, Chachi?'

'Never mind where,' she replied impatiently. 'It is true, what I have said, and that's why I say these *Firangans* will prove troublesome.'

'Now you are going too far, Chachi,' said Hafizullah. 'Upon my head, you are very careless in what you say. What charge can you bring against our guests here?'

'Well, when they first entered Javed's house, there was some excitement among the men in the neighbourhood.'

'Quite possibly,' said Hafizullah with sarcasm, 'your good husband was a little excited too, I suppose. Well, what came of it?'

'You are a funny boy, Hafiz!' she said mischievously, giving him a knowing wink in full sight of us. 'What are your intentions, eh?'

'You are behaving very stupidly today, Chachi!' said Hafizullah, growing impatient. 'What do you insinuate by that shake of your unbalanced head? I tell you again, be careful how you speak of Mariam and her daughter!'

'The boy stands as a champion of the white brood! Well, I have no patience with them.'

There was a pause in the contention. Mother, Anet and I had remained absolutely silent during this heated conversation; we were not in a position to say anything in our own defence, for we were in Qamran's house only on sufferance, and had no right to quarrel with anyone; and at the same time, we could not have improved on Hafizullah's performance.

Umda was bent on mischief and would not change the subject. 'My son has gone with the expedition. I hope and pray that he does not bring a *Firangi* female back with him.

Hafizullah was ready for her. 'No doubt your son will perform deeds of great valour on his expedition, but considering that it is only a few refractory landowners that they have been sent to quell, I don't think there is any chance of his finding any *Firangans* to come back with.'

Before Umda could take up the cudgels again, Hafizullah got to his feet and told her that it was time she returned to her own house; that he did not intend sitting by to hear us abused by her. But Umda was determined to have the last word.

'Great is the power of prayer,' she said. 'I have advised Khan-Begum to take ashes in her hand, and blow them towards these women so that they might fly away like this.' And throwing a pinch of dust towards us, she mumbled something under her breath.

It was too much for Hafizullah Khan. He rushed at Umda and dragged her out of the veranda. Then telling her to be gone, or he would be more rough with her, he returned and sat down near his wife, in a great rage.

The Rains

'It does not surprise me,' said Qamran, when she came home and heard of the quarrel between Umda and her son-in-law. 'Umda has too long and too venomous a tongue altogether. What business is it of hers that you should be my guests? She might have taken a lèsson from you in patience and forbearance. Son!' she said, addressing Hafizzullah. 'You need not have dragged her out. Nevertheless, it was noble of you to have taken the side of these unfortunate ones. Mariam, forgive her for her foolishness. She has only succeeded in giving the young an opportunity to jeer at her. In my house you will always be welcome.'

It was now the height of the rainy season, and heavy clouds were banking in the west. A breeze brought us the fresh scent of approaching rain, and presently we heard the patter of raindrops on the jasmine bushes that grew in the courtyard. It was the day of the monsoon festival observed throughout northern India by the womenfolk, who put on their most colourful costumes, and relax on innumerable swings, giving release to feelings of joy and abandon. Double ropes are suspended from a tree, and the ends are knotted together and made to hold narrow boards painted in gay colours. Two women stand facing each other, having taken each other's ropes by catching them between their toes. They begin to swing gently, gradually moving faster and higher, until they are just a brightly coloured blur against the green trees and grey skies. Sometimes, a small bed is fixed between the ropes, on which two or three can sit while two others move the swing, singing to them at the same time.

A swing having been put up from an old banyan tree that grew just behind the house, Badran and Hashmat, both dressed in red from head to foot, climbed on to it. Anet and I swung them, while Gulabia, the servant-girl, sang. When they came down we had our turn, and I found it an exhilarating experience, riding through the air, watching the racing clouds above me at one moment, and Anet's dark curls below me at the next. Removed for a while from the world below, I felt again that life could be gay and wonderful.

Mother's memory was stored with an incredible amount of folklore, and she would sometimes astonish our hosts with her references to sprites and evil spirits. One day Badran, having taken her bath, came out into the courtyard with her long hair lying open.

'My girl, you ought not to leave your hair open,' said Mother. 'It is better to make a knot in it.'

'But I have not yet oiled it,' said Badran. 'How can I put it up?'

'It is not wise to leave it open when you sit outside in the cool of the evening.'

'There are aerial beings called jinns, who are easily attracted by long hair and pretty black eyes like yours,' said Mother.

Badran blushed, her mother and husband both being present; and Qamran smiled at the recollection of her own youthful waywardness, when she made everyone believe that she was the object of a jinn's passion.

'Do the jinns visit human beings?' asked Hafizullah Khan.

'So it is said,' said Mother. 'I have never seen a jinn myself, but I have noticed the effect they have on others.'

'Oh, please tell us what you have seen,' begged Qamran.

'There was once a lovely girl who had a wealth of black hair,' said Mother. 'Quite unexpectedly she became seriously ill, and inspite of every attention and the best medical advice, she grew worse every day. She became as thin as a whipping-post and lost all her beauty, with the exception of her hair, which remained beautiful and glossy until her dying day. Whenever she fell asleep, she would be tormented by dreams. A young jinn would appear to her, and tell her that he had fallen in love with her beautiful hair one evening as she was drying it after a bath, and that he intended to take her away. She was in great pain, yet in the midst of her sufferings her invisible tormentor never ceased to visit her; and though her body became shrivelled, there shone in her eyes an unearthly light; and when her body decayed and died, her gorgeous head of hair remained as beautiful as ever.'

'What a dreadful story!' said Badran, hurriedly tying another knot in her hair.

Conversation then turned upon different types of ghosts and spirits, and Qamran told us about the *Munjia*—the disembodied spirit of a Brahmin youth who had died before his marriage—which is supposed to have its abode in a pipal tree. When the *Munjia* gets annoyed, it rushes out from the tree and upsets bullock-carts, *meanas* and even horse-driven carriages. Should anyone be passing beneath a lonely pipal tree at night, advised Qamran, one should not make the mistake of yawning without snapping one's fingers in front of one's mouth.

'If you don't remember to do this,' said Qamran, 'the *Munjia* will dash down your throat and completely ruin you.' Mother then launched into an account of the various types of ghosts she was acquainted with: the ghosts of immoral women—*churels*—who appear naked, with their feet facing backwards; ghosts with long front teeth, which suck human blood; and ghosts which take the form of animals. In some of the villages near Rampur (according to Mother), people have a means by which they can tell what form a departed person has taken in the next life. The ashes are placed in a basin and left outside at night, covered with a heavy lid. Next morning, a footprint can be seen in the ashes. It may be the footprint of a man or a bird or an elephant, according to the form taken by the departed spirit.

By ten o'clock we were feeling most reluctant to leave each other's company on the veranda. It did not make us feel any better to be told by Mother and Qamran to recite certain magical verses to keep away evil spirits. When I got into bed I couldn't lie still, but kept twisting and turning and looking at the walls for moving shadows. After some time, we heard a knocking on our door, and the voices of Badran and Hashmat. Getting up and opening it, we found them looking pale and anxious. Qamran had succeeded in frightening them, too.

'Are you all right, Khurshid?' they asked. 'Wouldn't you like to sleep in our room? It might be safer. Come, we'll help you to carry your bed across.'

'We are quite all right here,' protested Mother, but we were hustled along to the next room, as though a hand of ghosts was conspiring against us. Khan-Begum had been absent during all this activity (though she had been present during the story-telling), and the first we heard of her was a loud cry. We ran towards the sound and found her emerging from our room.

'Mariam has disappeared!' she cried. 'Khurshid and Anet have gone too!'

And then, when she saw us come running out of her own room, our hair loose and disordered, she gave another cry and fainted on the veranda.

White Pigeons

'You are bearing your troubles very well,' said Hafizullah to Mother one evening. 'You are so cheerful and patient, and you seem to look forward to the future with hope. And after all, what is the good of mourning for a past which can never return?'

'I doubt if there can be any improvement in their situation,' said Khan-Begum. 'Only yesterday the fakir was saying that the *Firangis* had been wiped off the face of the land.'

'I am not so sure of that,' remarked Hafizullah.

'Nor I,' said Qamran. 'The fact is, we do not get much news here.'

'Well, I can tell you something,' said Hafizullah. 'Though my uncle did boast the other day that there were no *Firangis* left, I overheard him whispering to Sarfaraz Khan that they were not yet totally extinct. The hills are full of them. My uncle was relating how Abdul Rauf Khan had gone on the morning of Id to pay his respects to Mian Saheb, the same fakir you speak of, and he was astounded by what the old man told him.

'What was it?' urged Khan-Begum.

'Abdul Rauf said that Mian Saheb was in a strange mood. He cast off the white clothes which he had been wearing during the past three months and, very suddenly, and without apparent reason, put on a black robe. Abdul Rauf and the others had gone to him to ask that he pray for the defeat of the *Firangis* before Delhi, but what do you think he told them?

Hafizullah paused dramatically, and both Qamran and Khan-Begum said at the same time, 'What did he tell them?'

'He told them that the restoration of the *Firangi* rule was as certain as the coming of doomsday. It would be another hundred years, he said, before the foreigners could be made to leave. "See, here they come!" he cried, pointing to the north where a flock of white pigeons could be seen hovering over the city. "They come flying like white pigeons which, when disturbed, fly away, and circle, and come down to rest again. White pigeons from the hills!" Abdul Rauf folded his hands and begged Mian Saheb to say no more. But the Mian is no respecter of persons, and his words are not to be taken lightly.'

* * * * * *

Our stay with Qamran was drawing to a close. We had passed almost the entire rainy season in the company of her agreeable household, and time had passed swiftly. We could not have received greater kindness or sympathy than we had been given by Qamran, and her son-in-law, Hafizullah. Javed Khan had been several times to see us—or rather, to see his wife and sister. Once or twice he had pressed Qamran to shorten our stay, but she did not want us to leave, and kept us on the pretext that we were sewing some things for her, which were not quite ready. He did not press her too much, as he knew that having both his wife and us under his roof did not make things easier for him.

Though appointed by the Nawab to a military command, we did not hear that Javed had engaged in any new or daring enterprise. His sacking of the Rosa Rum Factory had been his chief exploit to date, and that too had been done more for personal gain than from any other motive. He had shown no enthusiasm for the massacre at Muhamdi, where a company of sepoys had finished off the few Europeans who had managed to get away from Shahjahanpur. Now he limited his services to attending the Nawab's receptions, and to keeping him informed of news from Delhi and the whereabouts of stray refugees and surviors like ourselves. We heard, for instance, of the hiding-place of the

Redmans. A beggar woman happened to be passing before the house of the Redmans' old washerwoman, and stopping there to beg, recognized the tall, fair woman sitting in the yard.

'Who are you, eh?' she cackled. 'I know who you are! And where are your white husband and son?'

'Be off, *churail*!' said Mrs Redman. 'Go about your begging, and do not interfere with my affairs.'

Meanwhile the dhobi came home and, taking in the situation, told the beggar woman, 'How do you know she is a *Firangan*? She happens to be my sister-in-law.'

'Very fair for one of your caste!' said the old woman slyly.

'Ask any more questions and my washing-board will descend on your head!' threatened the dhobi. 'Be off, dead one!'

The beggar woman hobbled off, cursing both the dhobi's family and the Redmans, and made her way to Abdul Rauf Khan's house, where she informed him of what she had discovered. Abdul Rauf took his information to the Nawab, and suggested that he be permitted to capture the *Firangan*.

'That would be an adventure worthy of you,' said the amused Nawab. 'No doubt you would need an armed detachment to capture her. But I prefer not to hound these refugees, Khan Saheb. They have not done our cause any harm.' And he showed them the same forbearance that he had shown us.

******

The season of Moharram had come and gone. We did not even notice that it was over, for there were very few Shia families in Shahjahanpur, and the festival was not kept up with the same zeal that was shown in other towns. Unlike the Shia women, the Pathan women do not go into mourning during the ten days of fasting, nor do they remove their ornaments. Food and clothing were, however, sent to the nearest mosque to be distributed among the poor of the city.

Moharram over, it was decided that we should return to Javed Khan's house on Friday, the 4th of September.

The Impatience of Javed Khan

Poor Khan-Begum was to suffer many more pangs of jealousy before she could be done with us. On the same day that we returned to her house, Javed Khan took the opportunity to question Mother again, regarding her plans for my marriage.

'Tell me, Mariam, how much longer am I to wait?' he asked after dinner.

'What can I say?' sighed Mother. 'You ask me so often. I have already told you that I cannot give my daughter away without consulting my brothers. You had agreed to wait until the contest before Delhi was decided.'

'May the *Firangi* name perish, I say!' he exclaimed furiously. 'Surely your brothers have all been exterminated by now!' Then, his mood changing suddenly from anger to a brooding sullenness, he muttered to himself: 'Perhaps the fellow spoke the truth when he said, "Subedarji, will you reach Delhi at all?" For Ghansham Singh was not fated to set foot within the walls of the city. He fell at the Hindan bridge, when the *Firangi* army attacked the Bareilly brigade. He could not tell the King of our achievements here on the 31st of May. Well, I have done my part—and the sugar loaf solved my sherbet problem at Moharram. I would also have dealt well with that boy at Mangal Khan's, but the fool, Mangal, came between us and said he had adopted the boy as his own son. I never heard of a true believer adopting an infidel—a plague on them all!'

His face was dark and threatening as he went out of the house, and after a few minutes, we were startled by the screams of the boy Saifulla, Javed's half-brother, who had bumped into Javed in the lane and upon whom the Pathan was now venting his rage and frustration.

Javed Khan had stripped the boy to the waist, and taking out his horsewhip, had lashed the boy so severely, that the skin was actually torn from his back. Saifulla was laid up for several days, yelling from the pain which the festered parts gave him; but instead of softening toward him, Javed Khan threatened to repeat the flogging if the boy didn't stop groaning.

I have no doubt that it was Mother's disappointing answer that had driven Javed into a frenzy, and I suppose I should have been grateful that his passion had found an outlet on the back of his brother. Javed hated the boy for being the offspring of an illicit affair of his father's.

The same evening, Javed gave a further display of his savage disposition. Having enquired from the syce whether his horse had received its gram, and having been informed that Rupia, the servant-woman, had not yet ground it, he called the woman and demanded to know why the gram had not yet been ground.

'I was busy with other things,' she explained.

'Were you, you dead one?' he shouted fiercely, and seizing his whip again, laid it on her so violently, that she was literally made black and blue, and her torn and scanty clothes were cut to rags. She was bedridden for several days. Every one in the house went about in apprehension, wondering what Javed's next outburst would be like, but Mother could not bear to hear the groans of the woman and the boy. She had Zeban fetch some ground turmeric, which she heated on the fire and applied to the bruises. She attended to them for three days until their wounds began to heal.

One day Javed approached Mother again, and we were afraid there would be a repetition of his earlier display of temper; but he looked crestfallen, and was probably a little ashamed of his behaviour. He complained of having pains all over his body, and begged Mother to tell him of a remedy.

'You have been prescribing for those two wretches,' he said. 'Can't you give me something too?'

'What can I give you?' replied Mother. 'I am not a hakim. When I was in my senses I might have been able to think of something for your pain. You look very well, I must say.'

'I am not well,' said Javed. 'I cannot sit on my horse as well as usual. It is all due to my disregard for the wisdom of my betters: "Don't shoot on a Thursday." Last Thursday when I went out shooting, I saw a black buck and fired at it, but I missed, and instead, I hit a white pigeon sitting on a tomb. The pigeon flew into a bush, and I could not find it; but it must have been killed. I got nothing that day, and when I returned home in the evening, I felt exhausted and quite unable to use my limbs. I was as stiff as a dead one. Abdul Rauf was informed, and when he heard of what had happened he came to see me, very angry, because I had fired on the bird. "Pigeons," he said, "are people who come out of their graves on Thursdays for a little fresh air." Well, Abdul Rauf had me treated, shut me in a room, and eventually I came to myself. But. I have this swelling on my face, where the dead one must have slapped me.'

His face did appear to be slightly swollen; but, before Mother could take a closer look, Javed started at the sound of music in the street. His face underwent a violent change and, taking down his whip, he rushed out of the house.

There was a great deal of commotion outside, and then we heard the sound of someone shouting: '*Hai! Hai!* Save me, I am being murdered!'

We all looked at each other in wonder, and Khan-Begum said, 'It must be that boy who passes this way sometimes, singing and playing love songs on his flute. My husband swore, by the soul of his dead father, to flog the fellow within an inch of his life if he caught him singing before this house.'

'But what harm is done by his singing?' asked Mother.

'None that I know of. But in a Pathan settlement, no one is allowed to sing or play any instrument in the streets. Music is supposed to excite all sorts of passions, and so it is discouraged.'

'Still, I do not see what right our protector has to assault another in the street merely because he is singing and playing his flute. Is Javed not afraid that he might have to answer to the Nawab for his high-handedness?'

Khan-Begum began to laugh. 'The Nawab?' she said, 'Of what are you thinking, Mariam? Why should the Nawab care about it?'

A Visit from Kothiwali

It was the 13th of September, a Sunday morning, when the family barber brought a message from Kothiwali for Javed Khan. 'Your Chachi sends you her salaams, and says she intends to pay you a visit tomorrow.' To this Javed Khan sent the reply. 'It is my Chachi's house, let her come and throw the light of her presence on it.' Messages of this sort were always couched in extremely polite language.

The following morning Kothiwali arrived in her *meana,* attended by her servants. We were glad to see her again, as she was always so friendly.

'Now, Mariam, I have come to ask you to spend some time with me. I am seething with jealousy because you spent so much time at Qamran's house. Javed, you have no objection to my taking them with me?'

"It is all the same to me whether they stay here or go with you,' said Javed Khan with a shrug of his shoulders.

'Why so?' asked Kothiwali mischievously. 'I thought you were unhappy unless they were under your own roof?'

'True, but what good is it?' he said. 'My ambition was to possess the girl.'

'Well, she is in your possession now, isn't she?' said Kothiwali.

'Upon my head, you are exasperating!' exclaimed Javed. "So far as her presence in my house goes, she is in my possession, but what of that? I would marry her today, if it were not for her mother's procrastinations! Sometimes it is: "I have not consulted my brothers," as if she had any brother left to consult. Sometimes it is: "Wait until the fighting before Dilli is over," as if, even when it is over, it will make any great difference to people like us. It is foolish to expect that the *Firangis* will be victorious. Have I not seen a score of them running for their lives pursued by one of our soldiers?'

'Perhaps, but it is not always like that,' said Kothiwali.

'I wonder why your sympathies are with them, Chachi?'

'Well, they have always been quite good to me,' she replied. 'When my husband was killed by his enemies, it was the Collector who came to my house to condole with me, and it was he who saw to it that our fields were not taken from us. True, that was a long time ago. But I have no reason to wish them ill. At the same time, don't think I wish to run down the cause you have made your own—the rebel cause, I mean.'

'The *rebel* cause! Why do you always call it the rebel cause, Chachi?' Javed Khan looked very upset. 'Rebels against whom? Against aliens! Are they not to be expelled from the land? To fight them is not rebellion, but a meritorious act, surely!'

'Maybe, if it doesn't involve the murder of innocent women and children. But see how the *Firangis* are holding out before Delhi!'

'Enough, Chachi. Say no more, or you will rouse the demon in me. Let us not anticipate events. Delhi still stands, and Bahadur Shah reigns!'

'Nevertheless, I would advise you to take Mariam's suggestion and wait until the siege is raised. Be cautious, Javed, in your designs on this girl.'

'I have need to be, no doubt, after hearing about the example set by the Kanpur girl.'

'Oh! And who was she?'

'The General's daughter. A girl still beautiful at the age of twenty. She was saved from the massacre by Jamadar Narsingh, one of Nana Saheb's bodyguards, who would have liked to make her his wife. His intentions, like mine, were probably quite honourable, but Zerandaz Khan, another officer, stole the girl one night from the Jamadar's house, and treated her so savagely, that he roused in her all the pride and resentment of her race. For some time she concealed her feelings, but one night, when he was asleep, she drew his scimitar from under his pillow and plunged it into his breast. She then went and threw herself in a well. That was pluck and daring, wasn't it, Chachi? But,'—pointing at me, though looking away—'I have not even looked her full in the face, believe me!'

'Ah, you sly man!' said Kothiwali jestingly.

There was a pause at the end of which Kothiwali said, 'They may come with me, Javed, mayn't they? You are in a surly mood this morning.'

'Oh yes, take them with you,' he muttered sulkily. 'If they are happier with you, they may go with you.'

******

Seated in the same *meana* as Kothiwali, we were carried along to her house. I should really call it a mansion, because it was a large brick building with a high entrance and a spacious courtyard. There was also a set of glass-roofed chambers over the gateway, which the men used as retiring rooms; while the women's apartments were situated on the ground floor, and were cool and spacious.

The family consisted of Kothiwali, her daughter and two sons, one daughter-in-law, one son-in-law, and innumerable grandchildren. Kothiwali was the widow of a landed proprietor in the District, and must have been about forty years old when we knew her. She was tall, with black hair and eyes, a large mouth, small teeth, coloured black with *missi* and paan. She wore no trinkets except for a round silver bangle on each hand, and a plain silver ring on her right small finger. Her face was always cheerful, and she possessed great spirit. She commanded great respect from the rest of her community, who often came to consult her when in difficulty.

Mother soon became a favourite in the household, and so did Anet and I, but to a lesser degree. Kothiwali paid special attention to us. 'What quiet girls they are!' she would sometimes say. 'They never waste their time in idle talk.'

'Why not have the girls' ears and noses pierced?' She said to Mother one day.

'What would be the good when I have nothing to make them wear,' replied mother.

The lobes of our ears were already pierced, and I was glad I did not have to submit to having my nose pierced as well.

'I am glad you did not submit to Javed's request for your daughter's hand in marriage,' said Kothiwali. 'Had she been my daughter, I would never have agreed. Javed is very inconstant.'

'It would have been an incongruous match,' said Mother.

'My poor husband could never have imagined that she would be sought for by a Pathan as his second wife!'

Kothiwali's elder son, Wajihullah Khan, came in and sat down while we were talking. He was a young man of twenty-five, a hafiz—one who knows the *Quran* by heart—and regular at his prayers: it was he who gave the call to prayer in the neighbouring mosque. He was fair, of medium height, and quiet and respectful in his manner.

His usual haunt was the bungalow over the gateway, where he spent most of his time reading or playing chess—a game which is now losing much of its popularity. He came in with a friend named Kaddu Khan, a very handsome young man, who called Kothiwali Chachi. I think I recognized him as one of the band who had forced us to leave Lala Ramjimal's house. He was suffering from consumption in its first stage, and Wajihullah joined Kothiwali in begging Mother to prescribe something for him.

'I am not a doctor,' said Mother. 'I know the remedies for some minor ailments, but I very much doubt if I could help this boy.'

'No, do not refuse to do something for him,' urged Wajihullah. 'He is really a man of an adventurous spirit, though he has yet to gain fame for his achievements.'

'Do not make fun of the poor fellow,' said Kothiwali. 'He looks sufficiently depressed already.'

'No, I shall relate his worthy deeds to Mausi, before I ask her to give him something to improve his condition.'

Kaddu Khan now looked more dejected than ever and hung his handsome head in acute embarrassment.

'To begin with, Mausi, this is the gentleman who proposed to Nawab Qadar Ali to dig up the Christian graves for the treasure which, he was sure, was buried there.'

Kaddu Khan looked up and said, 'So I was made to believe. And the fox who gave me that information also told me that when a *Firangi* dies, two bags of money are buried with him.'

'And of course you believed that absurd story, and went about digging up their bones? Tell us what treasure you found!'

'We began digging at night,' said Kaddu Khan, deciding it would be better if he told the story himself. 'It was a moonlit night. There were three of us. I volunteered to go down into the grave and bring up anything valuable that I could find. To keep in touch with my comrades, we hammered a peg in the ground above and fastened a rope to it, and with its help, I slipped down. But imagine my horror when, instead of touching firm ground, I found myself hanging between heaven and earth! I let out a cry of distress. My comrades, instead of helping me out, thought the *Firangi* devils were after us, and instantly took to their heels, leaving me dangling over the grave.'

'A situation you had merited,' observed Wajihullah. 'But tell us how you got out.'

'I hung on to the rope and with a great deal of effort managed to raise myself to the bank. And now I tried to follow the example of my brave companions by making a run for it, but as I got up to do so, I felt a violent jerk around my waist and fell down again. Again I tried to get up and run, and again I was pulled to the ground. I was half-dead through fright, but I made one last lunge forward, and this time the wooden peg came up too, and I lost no time in taking to my heels. Chachi, that graveyard is full of *Firangi* devils!'

'What a thick-headed fellow you are!' said Wajihullah, enjoying himself immensely. 'One would think there would be some sense beneath that beautiful brow of yours. It was your waistband, Kaddu, that got hammered down with the peg. It left you dangling over the grave, and when you tried to run, it pulled you down again. It was only when you pulled the peg up that your cummerbund was loosened.'

Kothiwali and the rest of us had a good laugh at Kaddu Khan's discomfiture.

'It should serve as a lesson to you,' said Kothiwali, 'that all men are alike when the time comes to die. When you are dead would you like somebody to disturb your body in search of treasure? Treasure indeed! Even kings go empty-handed when they die. A child, when it is born, comes into the world with a closed fist, and the same hand lies open and flat at the time of death. We bring nothing into the world and we take nothing out!' At this juncture, Kaddu Khan's mother and sister joined us and, folding their hands to Mother, entreated her to do something for the youth.

They had conceived an exaggerated idea of Mother's powers of healing. All she told Kaddu to do was to take a dose of *khaksir* tea every six hours, and to abstain from acidic and hot food; and she told him to chew some fresh coconut every morning, drinking the juice as well. Kaddu Khan tried these simple remedies, and we heard that he eventually got better.

The Fall of Delhi

We were sitting in the veranda with Kothiwali when there was a disturbance in the next porch, where most of the men were sitting. Javed Khan had just ridden up, and had whispered something in Sarfaraz Khan's ear. Sarfaraz got up immediately and came and whispered something to Kothiwali. As soon as he had gone, Kothiwali turned to Mother and said, 'Well, Mariam, Delhi has been taken by the *Firangis*. What great changes will take place now . . .'

Our hearts leapt at the news, and tears came to our eyes, for a British victory meant a release from our confinement and state of dependence; but Delhi was a far cry from Shahjahanpur, and we did not give any expression to our feelings.

On the contrary, Mother took Kothiwali's hand and said, 'May you have peace out of it, too, Pathani.'

'Javed Khan will look quite small now, won't he?' said Kothiwali merrily. Apparently the news did not affect her one way or the other: she dealt in individuals, not in communities. 'But he has good reason to be worried. The *Firangis* will have heavy scores to settle in this city.'

******

The next day the menfolk held a long discussion. Some spoke of fleeing the city, others suggested that it would be better to wait and watch the course of events.

Sarfaraz Khan: 'Though Delhi has fallen to the *Firangi* army, it will be a long time before a small town like ours can be reoccupied. Our soldiers, who have been driven from Delhi, will make a stand at some other important place, Lucknow perhaps, and it will be months before we see a *Firangi* uniform in Shahjahanpur. Do not be in a hurry to run away, unless, of course, you have special reasons to be afraid of an avenging army . . .'

Javed: 'True, very true, *bhai.* I have done nothing to be afraid of. Have I, now? It's fellows like Abdul Rauf, who served under the *Firangis* and then threw in their lot with the sepoys, that are sure to be hanged. As for me, I never did take salt with the *Firangis.* If it comes to the worst, I shall ride across the border into Nepal, or take service in the Gwalior brigade.'

Sarfaraz: 'Oh, I'm sure you will. But why leave the city at all if there is nothing to be afraid of?'

Hafizullah: 'I saw some of our men who had returned from Delhi. They were lucky to get away. They had on only their tattered tunics and shorts.'

'Did they say anything of the fighting in Delhi?' asked Sarfaraz Khan.

'They told me that our army was not able to make much impression on the *Angrez* lines entrenched on the Ridge. There were many sorties, and during the last one, only a few days before the city was stormed, our men performed great feats of valour, but they were repulsed and cut down to the last man. The *Firangis* lost many men, too, but the victory gave them great confidence. When their storming parties approached the walls and blew open the Kashmiri Gate, their leader, Nikalsein, was seen waving his handkerchief on the point of his sabre from an elevated site. A ball struck him, and he fell. But his men forced their way through the city at the point of the bayonet, and Delhi is in *Firangi* hands again.'

'And what became of the King?' enquired Sarfaraz.

'He was made a prisoner, and his sons, who fled with him, were shot.'

'And so much for the rebellion,' said Sarfaraz Khan philosophically. 'The city of Delhi was a garden of flowers, and now it is a ruined country; the stranger is not my enemy, nor is anyone my friend . . .'

'Don't grow sentimental and poetic, Sarfaraz,' said Javed Khan irritably. 'Who was it who came to my house to kill certain people?'

'It was I,' said Sarfaraz. 'But did I kill anyone?'

Behind the Curtain

It was now winter, though the cold winds had not yet begun to blow. Mother sold two of the silver spoons from the jewel box which she had rescued from our burning house, and used the money to make quilts and some warm clothing to keep away the cold.

Ever since we had heard of the fall of Delhi, a change had come over our outlook and our expectations. We began to look forward to the time when Shahjahanpur would be reoccupied by the British—it would mean the end of our captivity which, though it had been made pleasant by Kothiwali and Qamran and their households, was not a state to which we could resign ourselves for ever; it would—we hoped—mean a reunion with other members of my mother's and father's families; and it would put an end to Javed Khan's plans to marry me. Our motives in hoping for the restoration of British authority were, therefore, entirely personal. We had, during the past months, come to understand much of the resentment against a foreign authority, and we saw that the continuation of that authority could only be an unhappy state of affairs for both sides; but for the time being it was in our interests to see it restored. Our lives depended on it.

But as yet there was no sign of the approach of British soldiers. We had no doubt that they would arrive sooner or later, but of course we did not speak on the subject, nor did we consider it prudent to show too great an interest in what was happening elsewhere. Of Kothiwali's sympathy we were sure, but we were afraid Javed Khan, in his defeat and frustration, might try to inflict some injury on us.

One day the mohalla sweeper, having taken ill, sent another girl to carry out her duties. The new girl recognized us as soon as she saw us, and a look of understanding passed between her and Mother. I remembered that she was called Mulia, and that she was the elder sister of a girl with whom I used to play when I was younger.

The latrine was the one place where we could manage any sort of privacy, and when Mulia went behind its curtain wall, Mother followed her.

'Mausi, you have no need to worry any more,' whispered Mulia. 'Delhi is taken, and your own people will be among us again. And I am to tell you that your brother is safe at Bharatpur. If you wish to send him a message, there is a person going on a pilgrimage to Mathura, and he will take your letter.'

Overjoyed at having met someone whom she knew and could trust, Mother agreed to make use of the messenger.

'But what am I to write the letter with?' she asked.

'Don't worry,' said Mulia, 'Tomorrow I will bring paper and pencil. Meet me here again.'

* * * * * *

We did not betray our feelings at this fortunate meeting, nor did anyone notice anything unusual about our behaviour. We did not even tell Anet or Granny about it, for fear that our hopes might be disappointed.

Next morning, keeping her promise, Mulia came again and waited for Mother behind the curtain wall. She handed her a scrap of paper and a small pencil, upon which Mother scribbled these words: 'I, Ruth, Anet, Mother, alive and well and hiding here. Do your best to take us away.'

She handed the note to Mulia, who slipped it into her bodice, Mulia then slipped away, leaving us in a state of suppressed excitement.

* * * * * *

It was early January, and we had been with Kothiwali for over three months. We had wanted for nothing but had, on the contrary, been treated with great kindness and consideration. We were rather disappointed when it was suggested that we shoud return to Javed Khan's house. He came himself and asked Kothiwali to let us go. Perhaps he still hoped that Mother might be persuaded to give her consent to my marriage—months had passed since the British had taken Delhi, but there were still no signs of their arrival in Shahjahanpur.

Khan-Begum was not exactly overjoyed at our return, and was still subject to fits of jealousy. There must have been a heated argument between her and Javed, because the morning after our arrival we heard him exclaiming to her angrily: 'I hate this constant nagging of yours.' She gave him some reply, which was followed by the slash of Javed's whip and a long silence.

He left the house without speaking to anyone, and only came back in the evening for his dinner. He asked Khan-Begum if she had anything to eat.

She replied: 'No, I am not hungry.'

'Then you had better sit down and eat,' he said, 'and don't put on any more of your airs.' She knew he was in a bad temper and had no wish to feel his whip again; so she did what he told her, though she remained glum and unfriendly until Kothiwali came and took us away again.

The Battle of Bichpuri

We were now in the middle of April 1858, and the hot winds of approaching summer brought the dust eddying into Kothiwali's veranda. The gulmohar tree outside the gate was aflame with scarlet flowers, and the mango trees were in blossom, promising fruit in abundance. The visits of Javed Khan to Kothiwali's house had of late become more frequent, and there were many whispered conversations between him and Kothiwali. We had no idea how we would fit in with their future plans should the British reoccupy Shahjahanpur.

One day Kothiwali received a visitor, a stranger whom we had not seen before. His name was Faizullah, and he too addressed Kothiwali as Chachi, though he was not related to her. He was a brash young man, and gave a vivid account of his experiences at Fatehgarh, from where he had just returned.

'So you were present at the battle of Bichpuri?' asked Kothiwali.

'Yes, Chachi,' he replied, 'and what a great battle it was! We fought the *Firangis* hand to hand, and made them feel the strength of our arms. I made a heap of the slain, and have brought with me a string of heads to present to the Nawab!'

'What a liar you are!' exclaimed Kothiwali.

'I swear by my head, Chachi!'

'How did a thin fellow like you manage to carry so many heads?'

'Why, I slung them over my saddle, and rode home in triumph.'

'And who was it who got the worst of the fight?'

'Why, the *kafirs*, of course, Chachi. We made a clean sweep of them,' and he passed the palm of his right hand over his left.

'Indeed!' said Kothiwali.

'There was not one man left, Chachi, so do you know what they did? They sent their women out to fight us!'

'This becomes more intriguing,' said Kothiwali. 'You are a gifted boy, Faizullah—you have a wonderful imagination! Tell us, what did their women look like?'

'Well, they were rather big for women. Some of them wore false beards and moustaches. But each one of them had a high skirt with a metal disc hanging down in front.' (It suddenly dawned on me that Faizullah was describing a Scots regiment of

Highlanders.) 'Such horrid-looking women, I assure you. Of course, there was no question of fighting them. I don't lift my hand against women, and out of sheer disgust I left the camp and came away.'

'You did right,' said Kothiwali. 'But will you not show us one of the *Firangi* heads you obtained?'

'I would be delighted to, Chachi but believe me, I have made a present of the whole string to the Nawab!'

Judging by the fact that Faizullah was safe at home instead of with a victorious army, we were fairly certain that they had been defeated by the British at Fatehgarh, and that it would not be long before Shahjahanpur was entered. This surmise was confirmed by Sarfaraz Khan who arrived at that moment and, giving Faizullah a look of scorn, said, 'So this warrior has been telling you of the *Firangi* heads he cut off! Is he able to tell us who cut off Nizam Ali Khan's head?'

This announcement produced quite a sensation, and Kothiwali jimped up, exclaiming: 'Nizam Ali killed! You don't mean it!'

Nizam Ali Khan was probably the Nawab's most valued official, a moderate and widely respected man. We had once had the lease of his compound, and had always found him courteous and friendly.

'But I do mean it,' said Sarfaraz. 'I have it on better authority than the chatter of this bragging lout. There is mourning in Nizam Ali's family, and both his sons have been wounded—one in the head, the other in the leg.'

Faizullah, abashed at being found out, sat gazing at the ground while his hands, which had been busy with the slings of his rifle, now lay motionless.

'The Nawab sent out a strong force under Nizam Ali with instructions to prevent the *Firangi* army from crossing the Ganga. But they were too slow and cumbrous, and the enemy had made two marches towards our city before Nizam Ali sighted them. The *Firangi* troops had just reached their camping ground when they noticed a cloud of dust rising on the horizon. Their scouts brought them the intelligence that the Nawab's army was marching upon them, and the cavalry was immediately ordered to remount and prepare for action. They attacked the Nawabi force before the latter had time to form, while the light guns raked them in the flank. Taken by surprise, our soldiers were demoralized. They were seized by panic, and broke and fled.'

'And what about Nizam Ali?' asked Kothiwali impatiently.

'He made a desperate attempt to keep his men together and to put up some sort of resistance, but his efforts were in vain. He could not bring any of his men together to make a stand. His gunners could not fire, as the fugitive soldiers surged from one part of the field to the other. Resolved not to survive this disgrace, Nizam Ali dismounted, and requested his servant to pass his sword through his body. But the servant would not. Then Nizam Ali rushed about madly and put his head into the mouth of a cannon, and ordered a gunner to apply a match and blow him to pieces. But the gunner refused. Poor Nizam Ali! He was about to stab himself with his poignard when the *Firangi* cavalry came thundering down like a torrent, sweeping all before them. A *sawar* belonging to De Kantzow's Horse recognized him—Nizam Ali's distinctive appearance could not be mistaken—and wheeling round, charged at him at full gallop and pinned him with his lance to the ground. And so ended the life of a man who possessed more determination and character than Abdul Rauf Khan, and who was the mainstay of the Nawab. With Nizam Ali gone, I doubt if the Nawab's government will last another week.'

'I am truly sorry to hear of his fate,' said Kothiwali with a sigh. 'But what became of his sons? You said that two of them were wounded.'

'Better that they had been killed by the side of their noble father. Why, they joined in the stampede and fled from the field of battle as fast as their horses could carry them, following the example of my friend Faizullah here. I have just left them beating their heads and yelling like old women over their fallen fortunes.'

'You are the bearer of serious news,' said Kothiwali. 'Unless I am very much mistaken, the *Firangi* army will soon be here. What will become of us, then?'

'They are marching this way, that is certain,' said Sarfaraz. 'There can be no doubt that the city will soon be reoccupied. We must think of how to save ourselves, because it is certain that they will order the city to be sacked, as was done at Delhi. It has become the custom now.'

'Allah forbid!' cried Kothiwali. 'Let us all meet this evening at my house and discuss measures for our safety. No time must be lost, because tomorrow the *Firangi* army is sure to be in the district, and the day after they will enter the city.'

And so Kothiwali, who had remained quietly at home all through the most violent stages of the revolt, now showed her qualities as a leader. She ordered these rough, disorderly men about as though they were children, and brought about a sense of organization where otherwise panic might have prevailed.

In Flight Again

That evening Kothiwali said to Mother, 'Well, Mariam, the *Firangis* are coming. I am glad that you are with me. Should it be necessary for us to flee the city, you will come with us, won't you?'

'Yes,' said Mother, 'for how will they know us for what we are? We have no one among them who would receive and protect us. From our complexions and our clothes they would take us for Mohammedan women, and we will receive the same treatment as your women. No, for the present we are identified with you all, and we must go where you go.'

When it was decided by Kothiwali that she and her family should flee Shahjahanpur, it was agreed by everyone that the rendezvous would be Javed Khan's house. We left for his house that same evening. There was Kothiwali's family; Qamran's family; and a doctor and his family, whom we had never seen before. Including Javed and his family, there were about thirty persons gathered at his house that evening, the 28th of April 1858. It was almost a year since we had left our own burning house behind. Before long, Javed Khan's house would be burning too. It did not make any sense at all; but I suppose war never has made sense to ordinary individuals.

There was, of course, no sleeping that night, for *meana* after *meana* kept dropping in till late, and there were whispers and secret consultations. The decision arrived at was that we should make our flight in a northerly direction, as the British force was marching from the south. And so, early on the morning of the 29th, long before dawn, the *meanas* began to fill up.

We had expected to get a seat in one of the *meanas* but soon they were all full and there was no room left.

Javed Khan came up to us and said, 'Mariam, you had better get into the doctor's bullock-cart. You will be quite comfortable there.'

There was no other choice; and so the four of us—Granny, Mother, Anet and myself—took our seats in the cart. Beside us were the doctor's wife, her brothers' wives, and their children. The party set off at once, the men riding ahead on their horses, while the *meana*-bearers trotted along at a brisk pace, and our bullock-cart trundled along in the rear.

After about two hours we reached the village of Indarkha, some eight miles out of Shahjahanpur. The sun was up, and when we raised the cloth which formed the roof of our cart, we were astonished to find ourselves alone, for the *meanas* and horsemen had all disappeared. It seemed that our driver had taken a circuitous route, and we had been left well behind. And there we were, in a strange village, and with companions who were unknown to us.

The doctor enquired for a vacant house where we could rest, but there was none to be had. The villagers were quite indifferent to our plight, and told us that we could not put up in the village. But the doctor grew bold, and brought them round to the notion that it was their duty to accommodate us all, whoever we were. Finally they told him: 'There really is no vacant house in the village, but there is one thing you can do. At the southern end of the village, just opposite the big banyan tree, a new house is being built. It is not yet complete, but it is habitable. You may occupay it and remain in it for a short time.' 'And so we gladly got down from our cart and entered a mud structure which consisted of a line of rooms at one end, a courtyard in front, and a wall all round.

We were, in a way, the guests of the doctor and his wife, and they were very kind to us. He was a Bengali Muslim, and had belonged to the Shahjahanpur regiment, but had severed his connection with it when it had marched out to Bareilly on the 1st of June 1857. Renting a house in the city, he soon acquired a reputation for possessing a healing hand and his practice flourished.

* * * * * *

The doctor's sisters-in-law now busied themselves with digging and setting up an oven. One of them lighted it and set a pot of dal on the fire, while the other kneaded flour and began to make chapattis.

That evening, after everyone had eaten, the doctor came in and sat down, and in very civil language asked Mother to tell him who she was and what her circumstances were. Mother told him our story, which aroused his sympathy and compassion.

'Do you think,' asked Mother, 'do you think that British authority will be restored again?'

'I do not know about the distant future,' he replied, 'but certainly their authority will be restored. But, I was going to say that now you are with us, I hope you will make yourself at home and command me in any way you please. We are all in the same boat at present, so let us help each other as best we can.'

Mother was touched by his expression of goodwill, and we remained with him that night and the next day. Long after sunset, when everything was still and the noisy birds in the banyan tree were silent, the doctor came to Mother and said, 'Javed Khan has come and he wants to speak to you.'

'Why has he come?' asked Mother. 'What further business has he with us?'

'He seems most anxious to see you,' said the doctor. 'He cannot come in here, but you can speak to him at the door.'

Mother went out to meet Javed Khan and I, being curious, followed her and stood in the shadow of the wall.

'Mariam,' said Javed, 'I have come to say that the *Firangis* have reoccupied Shahjahanpur. You will not, of course, go to them, but don't forget the protection you have received from me.'

'I will not forget it,' said Mother. 'I am grateful to you for giving us shelter. And I will never forget the kindness shown to me by Kothiwali and Qamran.'

'I have only one request to make,' said Javed, uneasily shifting his weight from one foot to the other.

'Yes, what is it?' asked Mother.

'I know that the time has passed when I could speak of marrying your daughter,' he said. 'It is too late now to do anything about that. But will you permit me to see her once more, before I leave?'

'What good will that do?' began Mother; but impelled by some odd impulse, I stepped forward into the light and stood before Javed Khan.

He gazed at me in silence for about a minute, and for the first time I did not take my eyes away from his; then, without a smile or a word, he turned away and mounted his horse and rode away into the night.

The Final Journey

The doctor spoke to Mother the next morning: 'I have heard that yesterday the British army entered Shahjahanpur and that a civil government has already been established. Won't you go to them now that order has been restored?'

'A good suggestion,' said Mother, 'but whom will we know among them?'

The doctor said, 'You will be known at once by your voice, your accent and your manner, and perhaps you will find that some of your own relatives have arrived and are looking for you.'

The doctor then went to the village elders and told them that Mother was a European lady who had escaped during the massacre, and that she and her family wished to go into Shahjahanpur. Now that civil authority had been restored, would anyone undertake to carry them into town on his cart?

'You are not telling us anything we don't know,' said the headman. 'As soon as they stepped down from your bullock-cart we knew who they were.'

'How did you know?' asked the doctor.

'You must take me for a pumpkin,' said the old man. 'Why, their very walk and their carriage indicated who they were. I marked their legs particularly. Those are not the feet, thought I, of women who go about barefoot. The way they treaded gingerly on the hot sand was proof enough. So they want to return to Shahjahanpur, do they? Well, I, Gangaram, shall take them in my own cart, and will reach them to any spot in Shahjahanpur where they wish to go. Tomorrow, in the morning, I shall be ready.'

* * * * * *

We put our few belongings together and the next day, at about ten, we got into Gangaram's bullock-cart and set out for Shahjahanpur.

Our journey was uneventful. We reached the town late in the afternoon, and asked Gangaram to take us to our old house, for we did not know where else we could go. As we halted before the ruins of our old house, Mr Redman came up and told Mother briefly of his own escape and his family's. He informed us that the British Commander-in-Chief had reoccupied the district, but had since then continued his march to Bareilly, leaving a small force under Colonel Hall to guard Shahjahanpur. He said the town was not quite safe yet, as the Maulvi of Faizabad was still in control of the eastern boundary of the district; and he advised us to take shelter in the quarters he was occupying with his family. Mother was reluctant to accept his invitation, but we were still homeless and without any male protection, and so we stopped for the night in the building in which the Redmans had taken shelter. Here we met a party of three men whom my uncle had sent from Bharatpur to escort us to him. One was a mounted orderly named Nasim Khan, and the other two were servants of the Maharaja of Bharatpur. We came to know that the note sent through Mulia had actually been delivered to my uncle, and he took immediate steps for our rescue. Mother wept to see the familiar handwriting of her brother, and to read his letter which was full of affection and anxiety for our welfare, and contained a pressing invitation to come to him at Bharatpur where, he said, she would find a home for the rest of her life.

This was on Sunday, the 3rd of May 1858. Next morning we were surprised to see Pilloo's mother arrive in our midst—without Pilloo! She looked so upset that we felt certain Pilloo had been killed; but when at last we got her to speak coherently, we discovered that Pilloo had decided to remain behind of his own accord! He has grown so attached to Mangal Khan that he refused to come away, and his mother had to leave without him, hoping he would relent and follow her. But he never did. He preferred the companionship of the Pathan, and continued to live with him and his family. We never did understand his behaviour.

While we were listening to Pilloo's mother's tale of woe, Mr Redman returned from a visit to Colonel Hall's camp and invited us all to sit down to breakfast. We had, however, scarcely eaten anything, when an alarm was raised that the rebel army, under the Maulvi of Faizabad, was crossing the Khannaut by the bridge of boats. Nasim Khan, my uncle's man, who had gone to bathe his horse at the river, came running back at the same time, with the report that the enemy had driven in the vedettes of the little force led by the Colonel, who had entrenched himself in the old jail. There was a smell of battle in the air. The sound of bugles, the neighing of horses, the clatter of riderless mounts dashing across the plain, the dull thump of guns, and the confused noise of men running in different directions; all these were unmistakable signs that a considerable force had attacked the small British garrison.

We had no time to lose if we were to save ourselves. Gangaram's cart was still at our disposal. Though Mr Redman assured Mother that there was no danger, she was determined to make for the countryside where she thought we would be safer. We all climbed into the cart: Granny, Mother, myself, Anet, Pilloo's mother, and Vicky, the Redman's daughter. We were scarcely out of the compound gate when we heard shouts, and, amidst a cloud of dust, some ten or twelve troopers of the rebel cavalry came riding at full gallop, flourishing their sabres in the air, and surrounded our cart. We heard one of them say: 'Here are some of them, let us finish them off!' We expected that at any moment they would tear the covering from over our heads and bury their shining blades in our bosoms. Little Vicky held her neck with both her hands, saying: 'Let us all put our hands round our necks so that only our fingers will be cut off and our heads will be safe!'

Everyone was unnerved except for Mother. With her eyes almost starting out of their sockets, her face haggard and lined after months of sorrow and uncertainty, she grasped the handle of her knife, while with her free hand she removed the covering and put out her head. Her expression was enough to frighten even these ruffians who were thirsting for our blood. They reined back.

'What do you want with us, young fellows?' said Mother. 'Is there anything unusual about seeing so many helpless females fleeing from the city to escape dishonour and death?'

They did not stop to hear any more. Believing us to be Muslim women escaping from the city, they turned about and tackled Nasim Khan, who was riding behind us. But he had the presence of mind to tell them that he was a soldier of the faith, and that the women in the cart were his relatives, leaving the city as the *Firangis* had occupied it.

After the troopers had gone, Gangaram came down from the cart, and folding his hands before Mother, exclaimed: 'Well done! You are weak in body, but you have the spirit of a goddess! I do not know of any other woman who could have dealt so well with those men.'

* * * * * *

Our adventures did not end there. Scarcely had we started moving again when, with a heavy thud, the cart fell down on its side. The axle had broken. There was no possibility of repairing it on the spot. We had to push on somehow, if we did not wish to fall in with another detachment of the enemy. The whirring and crashing of shells, the rattle of musketry, and the shouts of soldiers could be distinctly heard. We got down from the cart and, bidding goodbye to Gangaram, began to walk. We had no idea where we were walking, but it was our intention to get as far away as possible from the fighting.

After an hour of walking under the hot sun, we met a number of baggage carts passing along the highway. They belonged to the British army and were going, like ourselves, in the direction of Bareilly. One of the Sikh escorts saw us, and took pity on our condition. Mother had a high fever, and kept asking to be left alone by the wayside while we went on and found a place of safety. Nasim Khan dismounted and put her up on his horse, while he walked alongside, supporting Mother with his hands. At this moment another accident took place.

As Nasim Khan was dismounting, his pistol went off. This threw us all into panic once more.

Nasim Khan looked puzzled and turned round several times before he realized what had happened. 'Oh, how stupid of me!' he exclaimed. 'I had cocked it when we met the maulvi's men. But, as usual, it goes off only when the enemy is out of sight!'

The Sikh soldiers burst into laughter, and we could not help joining in, though our own laughter was rather hysterical. Then the Sikhs offered us a lift in one of the baggage carts, and Anet, Vicky and I gratefully accepted it, for we were completely tired out.

We journeyed on like this for another three or four miles until we reached a small village where we were offered shelter. As it was now afternoon, and there was no shelter in the baggage cart from the blazing sun, we were only too glad to accept the villagers' hospitality.

Two days later, having hired a cart, we proceeded towards the south and, avoiding the main highway, reached Fatehgarh after four days. There we joined up with Mr Redman's party; and Mother called on the Collector, who gave her some 'succour-money', which enabled us to continue our journey to Bharatpur in comparative comfort. Ten days later we were in the home of my uncle, where we found rest, shelter and comfort, until a rumour that a rebel force was about to cross the territory threw us all into a panic again. It was only a rumour. But the trials of the past year had made such an impression on my mind, that I was often to wake up terrified from nightmares in which I saw again those fierce swordsmen running through the little church, slashing at anyone who came in their way. However, our troubles were really over when we arrived at Bharatpur, and we settled down to a quiet and orderly life, though it was never to be the same again without my father.

We did not hear again of Lala Ramjimal and his family. We would have liked to thank him for his kindness to us, and for risking his own life in protecting us; but beyond the knowledge that he had settled with his family in Bareilly, we received no further news of him.

We heard that Kothiwali and Qamran and their families eventually returned to Shahjahanpur, after life had returned to normal. But Javed Khan disappeared and was never seen again. Perhaps he had escaped into Nepal. It is more probable that he was caught and hanged with some other rebels. Secretly, I have always hoped that he succeeded in escaping. Looking back on those months when we were his prisoners, I cannot help feeling a sneaking admiration for him. He was very wild and muddle-headed, and often cruel, but he was also very handsome and gallant, and there was in him a streak of nobility which he did his best to conceal.

Notes

Pathans formed thirty per cent of the Muslim population of Shahjahanpur (Muslims forming twenty-three per cent of the entire population) according to the 1901 census. Most were cultivators, although many were landed proprietors of the district. (True Pathans are descendants of Afghan immigrants.) 'Their attitude during the Mutiny cost them dear, as many estates were forfeited for rebellion.' (*Gazetteer*)

Most of the rebel leaders were either killed or brought to trial, and in all cases their property was confiscated. Ghulam Qadir Khan died shortly after the reoccupation and his estates were seized.

'The number of Muslims whose services (to the British) were recognized was extremely small, as, apart from the two men who sheltered their Eutopean kinsman, Mr Maclean, in pargana Tilhar, the only persons recognized were Nasir Khan and Amir Ali of Shahjahanpur, who buried the bodies of the Englishmen murdered on the occasion of the outbreak, and Ghulam Husain, who saved the commissariat buildings from destruction and for some time protected several Hindus on the district staff.' (p. 150, *Gazetteer*, 1900)

'At Jalalabad, the tehsildar Ahmed Yar Khan at once showed his sympathy with the rebels by releasing several criminals under arrest. On the arrival of Ghulam Qadir at Shahjahanpur, the tehsildar was raised to the dignity of *nezim*, but his tyranny aroused the resistance of the Rajputs of Khandar and other villages.' (p. 248, *Gazetteer*)

'Mr Lemaistre, a clerk in the Collector's office, was killed in the church, and the fate of his daughter is unknown.'

(*The Meerut Mofussilite*, 1858)

The city was populated by a large body of Afghans sent there by Bahadur Khan (a soldier of fortune in the service of Jehangir and later Shahjahan), at that time serving beyond the Indus. The story goes that these Afghans belonged to fifty-two tribes and that each had its own mohalla, many quarters of the city to this day being named after Pathan clans.... the history of the town and of Bahadur Khan's family is told in an anonymous work called the *Shahjahanpurnama* or the *Anhar-ul-bahr*, written in 1839, and also in the *Akbar-i-Muhabbat* of Nawab Muhabbat Khan.

I first heard the story of Mariam and her daughter from my father, who was born in the Shahjahanpur military cantonment a few years after the Mutiny. That, and my interest in the accounts of those who had survived the 1857 uprising, took me to Shahjahanpur on a brief visit in the late 1960s. It was one of those small U.P. towns that had resisted change, and there were no high-rise buildings or blocks of flats to stifle the atmosphere. I found the old church of St Mary's without any difficulty, and beside it a memorial to those who were killed there on that fateful day. It was surrounded by a large, open parade ground, bordered by mango groves and a few old bungalows. It couldn't have been very different in Ruth Labadoor's time. The little River Khannaut was still crossed by a bridge of boats.